THE VILLAGE HEADMASTER

ANEZI OKORO

Table of Contents

1

End of an Era

After the Assembly *for the* end of term, the school compound was like a *besieged* camp. Some pupils hurried to get out of the compound before one teacher or another caught them to send them on an *errand* or give them odd jobs to do. Parents and guardians rushed in to collect the younger children. Class monitors and teacher's servants dashed about between the classrooms and Teachers' Quarters carrying books and other personal belongings.

The rush raised *a cloud of dust* in the compound. The mid-morning air filled with *discordant* music. While some pupils sang or whistled or hummed the prayerful parting hymn: *'God be with you till* we *meet again'*, others preferred the more triumphant: "Holiday is coming..... No more morning bells... No more teachers' calls..." Above the music rang *boisterous* calls between friends and relations.

For the moment, the Central School Amanzu appeared to have *lost its head,* even though the iron discipline of the outgoing Headmaster, Mr Augustus U.G. Offor, had only been lifted a few minutes before.

As Ishmael Kanu, a Standard Two pupil, was running towards the east gate, his friend Olatunji Johnson called out: "Ishie, not staying on to see off the old H.M.?"

"No, thanks. I'm going to my fishing lines. The fish won't wait, and this is the holidays."

"But Oh! The poor old H.M! You may not see him again," Olatunji pleaded.

"He's not going to die, is he? Besides, who wants to see him off? I am still *seeing stars* after the beating he gave me last week."

"All right then, I'll report you to our class monitor. Our teacher said we should all stay behind to see the old man off. You heard him."

"Go ahead and report me to the H.M. himself. He can come from Afara to flog me next term. You are just jealous, Tunji, because you can't fish. I am going. Goodbye!"

Olatunji ran back to join some of his other classmates who were heading for the Headmaster's house near the south gate of the compound. There the teachers and some of the bigger boys were helping to pack luggage into the lorry which was provided by the grateful people of Amanzu for Mr Offor's journey to his new school. On the front and both sides of the lorry was splashed, in red and yellow, the name of the lorry **ARMA*GEDDON*.** Some pupils standing by *teased* one another with the spelling and pronunciation of the word.

"Come on, tie those yams properly, you clumsy fool," Mr Offor bawled at one pupil as he struggled to tie yams to one side of the lorry.

"Yes, Sir," the boy answered. It was the only possible reply to the outgoing Headmaster even during the holidays.

The creaky old lorry was already overloaded. There was no room inside for the yams, and the pupils were helping Mr Offor's servants to tie them to the right side of the lorry. The whole of that side of the lorry looked like a rack in a yam barn. On the left side of the lorry, Mr Offor's bicycle had already been securely fastened. Some newly made brooms, wooden pestles, machetes and hoes.

As Mr Offor shouted at one boy after another, Olatunji wondered if Ishmael was not right after all. Why waste goodwill on an old man who bullied everybody?

"*Come* on, *tie those* yams *properly*, you

clumsy fool"

Suddenly the fowls in the baskets on top of the lorry burst onto a chorus of *cackling* as if in protest. What appeared to have angered them soon became obvious. Matthew, the leader of the committee of Church Elders, arrived with three more goats and he was followed by people carrying yams, coco-yams, fowls and other gifts. The people of Amanzu seemed determined to show Mr Offor that they loved him more than they loved themselves. The giving away of precious yams during the planting season was a true sacrifice.

The fowls might well have wondered where the new arrivals would find room on or around that lorry. So did Mr Joseph Mozie who was Mr offor's assistant and the newly appointed Headmaster. In his quiet way, he was organizing the loading of the lorry and, as Matthew approached, Mr Mozie went to meet him. They went together to join Mr. Offor.

"I am sorry, H.M., that we have to bring these things in bits and pieces," Matthew apologized. "You know what our people are like. They may have a whole year in which to do something, but it is bound to be done at the last moment. However, their hearts are with you, and they wish you nothing but the best."

"Thank you, my dear friend Matthew," Mr Offor responded. "You have been wonderful. Your people have been *magnificent,* but some of the people who brought these gifts must stay around in case the lorry cannot take everything. It may be necessary for them to carry the rest on their heads to my new station. The way that lorry is groaning, I cannot see it making two journeys."

Mrs Amadi and Mrs Onuoha, two of the Women's Guild leaders, arrived at the head of a women's *delegation*. Most of the women's gifts had been brought the day before, and the delegation had come only to say: "Farewell" to Mr and Mrs Offor.

Stanislaus Igiri, the public letter writer, *breezed* in on his bicycles and parked in the shade of one of the mango trees. Stanislaus was at his *impeccable* best, white shoes and white hose. He was lithe in build and of a light complexion, his black hair combed neatly forward. His shirt pocket was studded with multi-coloured pens and always carried books. It was difficult not to notice Stanislaus when he arrived.

"Good day, Head! Good day one and all! And a happy holiday!" Stanislaus hailed, extending his greeting to everyone around." And how goes the loading?"

The last thing Mr Offor wanted was to be *drawn into conversation* with Stanislaus. He disliked Stanislaus who, when he was a court interpreter, had been imprisoned for taking bribes in order to distort interpretations. He disliked Stanislaus even more because of his mischief-making as a public letter writer. Stanislaus exploited the people's illiteracy, distorted their letters and telegrams, misrepresented facts to them and drove them into the unwholesome habit of frequent petition writing. Stanislaus, however, knew where he stood with Mr Offor and did not lose sleep over it. He received a number of "Good mornings" from the crowd and joined them quite happily.

"Where's my namesake, Stan? He asked, looking round for Mr Offor's third son, Stanley. "Oh, there you are, Stan. Here's a couple of little books for you to read on the way if you can *rub the dust out of* your eyes,

"Let's see those books," Mr Offor ordered. He snatched the two books from Stanislaus as he was about to give them to Stanley, and examined them, scowling as he did so. One *book* was *Arabian Nights*, and the other was *King Solomon's Mines*. Both were good, clean, entertaining books.

Mr Offor nodded his thanks to Stanislaus and handed the books to Stanley. The boy *jumped for joy*. The onlookers thanked Stanislaus for his present. Some of the school children *clustered* around Stanley to see his new books. The loading continued.

Stanislaus moved round, chatting amicably with everyone. He had an engaging manner and sounded so knowledgeable that it was difficult not to enjoy his company. But he had no luck with Mr Mozie.

"Good day, Mr Headmaster-Designate," Stanislaus greeted him.

"Good morning to you," Mr Mozie replied curtly.

"You are no doubt looking forward to your new assignment.'

"Yes, thank you."

"I am sure that the pupils and the people will like you for your gentleness," Stanislaus said in a very low tone barely above a whisper.

"Maybe, if you would be kind enough to allow them," Mr Mozie answered.

"Oh heavens! It will have nothing to do with me. I don't mind what happens. I like everyone."

As Mr Mozie walked away to continue his supervision of the loading, Stanislaus smiled to himself, drew one of the Committee men aside and asked him *confidentially*: "How do you take the Headmaster's transfer?"

"It's terrible!" the man exclaimed. Really awful! Amanzu will never recover from this blow. The place will never be the same again."

"Quiet! They will hear us," Stanislaus *cau*tioned. "You know that Mr Offor is going to take over from Mr Obioma who is going to be trained as a Pastor."

"So I hear, but why don't they send a respectable man as Headmaster instead of promoting this inexperienced, unmarried bookworm who does not know how to mix with our people. He does not know where any of us live."

"Precisely! That's the trouble," Stanislaus agreed, delighted to discover a ready *ally*. "You know, of course, about the letter which the Committee is writing to the Reverend William Jones, the Manager of Schools, in praise of Mr Offor."

"Of course I do. Mr Offor is a wonderful man. No praise is too great for him," the Committee man answered.

"You are perfectly right. But do you know what I think?"

"No! What is it?"

"Don't you think you should add in that letter the feelings you have just expressed; that you would prefer another Headmaster to this Mr Mozie?"

"Can it be done?"

"Sure! Why not?"

"Then, let's do it," the man said excitedly.

"Quiet!" Stanislaus cautioned again. They will hear us. My fear is that your Committee leader, Matthew, will not agree. He always talks of goodness and fairness and that kind of nonsense as if this world was heaven itself. Can you promise me that you will work on other Committee men so that they may agree to do this? It will be for your own good, you know. Otherwise the glory of Amanzu will soon become something of the past. There is nothing like a strong Headmaster."

"I promise."

You all have equal rights in that Committee, you know." "Do we?"

"Of course you do. And if you can do this, I promise to read and write all your letters and telegrams free of charge from now on."

"Oh, thank you. That will be wonderful," the man said, thinking about all the money he might save.

"Shall we then meet in the tailor's house after the headmaster has gone? The tailor is a good man. We can count on him."

Stanislaus gave the Committee man a *con*spiratorial wink and moved on to find himself face to face with Miss Comfort Chima. The young lady teacher was coming out of the Headmaster's house carrying food for the journey. Beside her was her pet pupil, Abigail Onuoha, who carried the Headmaster's baby son on her back.

"Ah, I haven't paid my respects to the great Miss Comfort Chima. *Comment* ca va, *Mademoiselle*?" he asked, trying out with his French.

"Very well, thank you, "Miss Chima replied.

"Now that Mr and Mrs Offor are leaving, where will you live? Will you be returning to your old school or are you going to stay here?" Stanislaus asked.

"Oh, I think I will stay here? Any *objection*?"

"Of course not. On the contrary, I am delighted to know that you are not going to *deprive* Amanzu of the charm you brought to it. I feel certain that the same goes for everybody here in this village. As the first lady teacher here, you have been a *boon,* and Miss Hill's loss has become our great gain."

"So you know about Miss Hill?" Miss Chima asked.

"Have a *heart,* Miss. What do you take me for? Of course I know what led to your coming to teach at Amanzu. The two top classes in the Girls' Demonstration School in Amaoji where you were teaching were closed because most of the girls in those classes got married. The Headmistress, Miss Hill, took up the matter with the Reverend William Jones, but could do nothing to recall the girls who had already gone into various fattening rooms in preparation for their weddings. Have I got all the facts wrong? Miss?"

"No, you haven't."

"Of course not. I move about quite a lot you know, and I keep my eyes and ears open," Stanislaus boasted, and then looked round to see who else he could talk to.

The fowls on the basket on the top of the lorry let out another burst of cackling.

"Silence, you jealous hearts!" Stanislaus commanded.

A temporary rack had just been put on top of the lorry to *accommodate* more loads. The driver's assistant was up there tying a new basket of fowls which had arrived late. With what was still lying about, it looked as if there would be as much luggage on the top of the lorry as there was inside it.

At last the loading was completed but, as was feared, some luggage remained. Matthew had no difficulty in getting volunteers to carry what was left on their bicycles. The bicycles were quickly loaded and the travelling party was ready.

Mr Obiako, the Church teacher, called everybody together and prayed that 'Armageddon' should take Mr and Mrs Offor and their travelling companions safely to their destination, and that the bicycle riders should not break their necks on the way.

Then came the exchange of parting greetings amidst much hugging and hand-shaking and, in some cases, sorrowful head-shaking too.

The bicycle squad set off first in order to avoid the inevitable dust-screen behind the moving lorry.

Mr Offor ordered his Children and servants into the back of the lorry and his wife, with the baby boy, into the front. Then he began a final round of hand-shakes and parting remarks.

"Thank you, my dear friend, Matthew, for all you have done for us. Look after our flock and our Committee. Help and defend the new Headmaster."

"By God's help, H. M., I will. Goodbye, and don't forget us."

"Joseph, I trust that, as Headmaster, you will make Amanzu Central School the best in the District. Good luck."

"Thank you, Sir," said Mr Mozie. "We shall do our best to maintain the high standard you have set *for* us."

Mr Offor had a word for everyone- Committee men, women, teachers, townspeople and pupils. He was about to enter the lorry when Stanislaus stopped him.

"What, H.M., not even a word or a handshake for me?"

"Okay, goodbye, Mr Igiri, and don't you go poisoning the minds of the good people of Amanzu against Mr Mozie, the new Headmaster."

"Me? Never! Safe journey, H.M., and don't do anything I wouldn't do." Stanislaus said good-humouredly.

There was a brief silence. The lorry driver, a burly young man with the muscular arms of a blacksmith, wiped his sweaty brow on his sleeve and then climbed into his seat. He leaned out to ask if all who were travelling had taken their seats.

"Sure!' Fire the engine and let's be off!" one of Mr Offor's children shouted from the back.

The driver tried the kick starter in the hope rather than the belief that the lorry would start. After three *futile* kicks, he drew the starting-handle from under his seat and tossed it into the waiting hands of his assistant who had already jumped down from his *perch* in the tailboard of the lorry. Then the battle started. 'Armageddon' had stood there overnight. The assistant pushed the shaft of the crank through the hole beneath the radiator, and began heaving. The engine coughed and sputtered but refused to start. When the assistant got tired, everyone around took turns at trying to start the engine. In the end, the driver himself had to jump down and do the cranking. He handed the steering-wheel over to Mr Offor, who had never driven a motor vehicle, and asked him to assist by pressing the accelerator pedal gently. This brought out beads of sweat on the poor Headmaster's face and a roar of laughter from the crowd. No one came to any harm and the driver and Mr Offor between them were able to make the mighty engine *roar* into *life*.

The crowd cheered. The passengers returned to their seats. The driver climbed in. He mopped his brow once more with his sleeve, and revved the engine hard and long to make sure that it would not *stall* again. The front of the Headmaster's house went black with the cloud of smoke from the exhaust pipe. The lorry *lumbered* forward down the school compound and onto the road.

Meanwhile the teachers and pupils and others in the send-off party had dashed across the compound to continue their waving and cheering until "Armageddon" was out of sight, swallowed up by the dust cloud which it raised.

2

The First Steps

Mr Mozie spent the first week of the holidays in Amanzu, taking stock of the school which fortune was now *entrusted* to his care. He waded through files, studied account books and registers, examined syllabuses, books, teachers' notes, examination results, and any material which promised information on any aspect of school life in Amanzu.

Then he spent the next few days in his hometown, Awka, not looking for a wife as his *adversaries* in Amanzu thought he should, but gathering his thoughts on how to *tackle* his difficult but interesting assignment. He had thought about Mr Offor's speech to the School on the last day of term.* It was not an untrue or even an *exaggerated* picture which Mr Offor had painted, but he believed it was wrong to lay the blame for the failure entirely at the pupils' door rather than at the staff's. He preferred to think that the fault lay equally with the staff, and that the staff must find a remedy for it.

Mr Offor's *castigation* had been a great help, much more help than his friendly handover talks and notes. It had helped Mr Mozie find a basis for his ideas on how to put things right. He made *a detailed analysis of* the problems as he saw them, and prepared a possible programme of *reform* by stages over the next year or two. He prayed for cooperation from his colleagues and for wisdom to find solutions to the problems ahead. Next he wrote to all the teachers asking them to return to the school a couple of days early. He proposed to them that they should hold a Staff Meeting on the last Friday of the holidays so as to be properly ready for the return of the pupils on Monday.

He spent the next week visiting old college friends in Enugu and Onitsha, away from all his thoughts and plans. They swopped stories about the various places they had worked in and news of other friends and rambled on about life in general. He enjoyed with them the atmosphere of these comparatively *sophisticated* rapidly developing townships.

A week of that was enough for him. He returned to Awka for Easter with his family, helped with the house repairs and advised about farming. There were a number of internal *squabbles* which needed his *intervention*, a backlog of funerals to attend and. money to be given to the *bereaved,* and also some friends and some old folk to visit. Holidays in one's home town could be exciting and exhausting, but Mr Mozie did not mind these things. He believed in them and enjoyed doing them. Attention to these details, he felt, made the inevitable break-up of village life, brought about by education, more acceptable to the older folk.

He travelled through Enugu back to Amanzu on the Monday of the last week of the holidays. His mother provided a great deal of food for him to take back to Amanzu. He had enough yams to last him most of the term, garri, sliced cassava, rice, dried fish, dried meat, oil, pepper, salt, kola-nuts for entertainment and almost every sort of food he needed.

The school compound was almost *deserted*. Only Mr Obiako, the Church teacher, and his family remained. They received Mr Mozie *enthusiastically* and gave him a meal in their house before he settled down. Mr Mozie moved into the Headmaster's house which was now his own.

***"My* dear *colleagues, you* realize.......**

The meeting on Friday was a Staff Meeting
with a difference. Mr Mozie made it a
discussion, the general theme being that of
teamwork. He chose the Standard Six classroom
in preference to his office for this first meeting
and was there early to welcome the staff one by
one as they arrived.

Miss Chima came early. She had spent her
holidays with her parents in Bende and visited
Miss Hill on a day trip shortly after Easter. For
the new term her parents had arranged that she

should live with Mr and Mrs Obiako now that the Offors, with whom she had lived before, had gone. She therefore arrived for the meeting with Mr Obiako.

Mr Mozie's introductory speech was direct and *to the point*. After formally welcoming them and saying that he hoped they had all had a good holiday, he went on: "My dear colleagues, you realize no doubt that our great friend Mr Offor's speech at the end of last term was a challenge to us all. His speech was *scathing* and *down*-to-earth, as well it might be. It was a challenge then. It remains a challenge today, and I propose with your kind cooperation to take up that challenge here and now.

From his quotation: "The son whom his father loveth he chideth', which you will remember, the spirit of his speech must be obvious. Mr Offor, if I read him right, did not excuse himself from blame. When he *chastized* our pupils, he was chastizing us. To be strictly accurate, he was condemning our system of work in this school. Poor students can only be the products of a poor system. Fortunately, he also offered us in his speech the very bricks with which to rebuild. He spotlighted our main deficiencies. We have merely to repair these deficiencies, and we shall be well on our way to achieving success. But piecemeal patching is a *laborious* and unreliable way of making progress. Better than this is the path of recasting our concept of the upbringing of these children, teaching being only one aspect of that upbringing, in this we may be guided by the following-principles.

The first is the realization that the most important person in this school is not the Headmaster, not any of the other teachers, not even the Committee men, but the humble pupil. We are all here because of him and not him because of us. His interest therefore comes first and ours, last; his happiness before our own.

At this a slight gasp was heard from one or two members of staff. Mr Mozie ignored them and continued: "All the other principles *stem* from this one. We should strive to ensure that the pupil's faith in the school is total and *unflagging*. In this way we shall make him look forward to class work not with jitters but with joy; regard manual work as *dignified* and not *degrading*; face outside competition with the will to win."

Mr Mozie's tone was *conversational*. He was not looking for applause, and just as the other teachers thought that he was going to lay down the rules on exactly what they were to do, he stopped and asked: "What do you think, lady and gentlemen?"

They were not used to being asked for their ideas. The good old H.M., Mr Offor, told them what there was to do, and that was that. They shifted uneasily in their seats. No one was prepared to start. It was not that they held Mr

Mozie *in awe*, but this sort of discussion needed getting used to.

Mr Obiako broke the silence eventually. "That speech of the old H.M. hurt me," he began. "But as you rightly said, H.M., his intention was good. He wanted to *prick* us *into action.* I would give my heart to see this school become a happier place for our pupils. I'll agree with whatever the H.M. wants us to do," He looked round and asked *genially:* "Does anyone disagree?"

No one disagreed. In short statements they all supported Mr Mozie's general ideas.

Miss Chima added that the principle of: "Students first" was one which operated in the Girls' Demonstration School. A few eyes were turned disapprovingly in her direction as if to say: "None of that Girls' School stuff here, Miss," but no one wanted to start on the wrong foot with the new H.M. and a quarrel with Miss Chima would surely be a bad start.

Agreement on general principles was one thing, but they still had *to hammer* out the details. Mr Mozie calmly and *unobtrusively* steered them through the plan he had drawn up. He did not *ram* the *points* down their throats, but rather made them introduce those he had in mind.

The *abolition* of caning during lessons was hotly contested by some, notably Mr Okehi, the Standard Two teacher. He argued that it was impossible to teach without the cane, and that the pupils could not learn their lesson without it. In his time, he said, he was "flogged from Infants One to Standard Six," and did not see why he should not be allowed *revenge*.

Surprisingly, old Mr Obiako was for abolition. Miss Chima was staunchly behind the idea; Mr Ibe quickly fell in with them. It was agreed to give it a trial.

Caning for truancy, deliberate lateness, wanton rowdiness in class, destructiveness and other misbehaviour was to remain.

One by one they discussed all the points raised, and drew up a plan of reorganization. It took them until well past lunch time.

At the end Mr Mozie thanked them sincerely for their co-operation and for their invaluable contributions. He dismissed them with the *exhortation* that this project of rebuilding the school system for the betterment of the pupils and ultimately of themselves was their target as a team and not his as an individual. He believed, he added, that the results would give all of them much more joy in the long run than they could then imagine. It was not going to be easy. No worthwhile achievements ever came easily.

3

The New Term

Palm Sunday, Good Friday and Easter had all come and gone while the pupils were on holidays. They had all enjoyed the festivities at home, but the younger ones missed the fun of making and flogging the daylights out of the *effigy* of Judas Iscariot for his everlasting sin of betraying Jesus for thirty pieces of silver nearly two thousand years before. If, as often happened, Good Friday had come during term, they would have made a large effigy looking like the teacher they disliked most.

When school resumed, it was about: 'Judas' that Ishmael asked Olatunji, because Olatunji had taught them a beautiful marching (or dragging) song which they sang as they dragged 'Judas' about and flogged revengefully.

Judasi...Ole!

Judasi... Ole!

Opa Jesu je...

Jadas was a thief. He killed

Jesus and ate.

Ole! Ole! Ole!

Judasi......Ole!
Judasi.....Ole!!

"Tunji, did you have 'Judas' during your holidays?" asked Ishmael.

"Oh yes, of course. Good Friday without 'Judas'can you imagine that? All the boys in the Railway Compound built a giant one. We dragged him round the Compound and into the station, and even along the rails for miles and miles," he exaggerated. "You know, on Good Friday there are no trains, so we weren't afraid of anything. By the time we came back, we had only the string and a bit of Judas' head left. The sacking and the stuffing had gone. We beat him, brother, we beat him!"

Ishmeal was very jealous.

"I wish I had visited you on that day, Tunji," he sighed. "You know, the boys in our village are very foolish. After service on Good Friday, they never play 'Judas'. They don't know the song. My silly brother Aaron doesn't even remember it, though you taught the whole class the song. Did you really drag him for miles and miles? You lucky thing!"

"Well, not really miles, Ishie, but we certainly dragged him a long way, past the first and second railway points on the south side, the Port Harcourt side, of the station. It was fun. You know...."

"All right, Tunji, that's enough. I hope next year's Good Friday will fall in term time. Remember, if it doesn't, you must remind me in time so that I can visit you on that day. *It's a bargain,* otherwise, no more dry fish or meat from me, agreed?"

"Sure, I'll remember, Ishic."

Mr Mozie was one teacher short because the new one promised by Mr Dewar had not arrived. He had no choice but to make do with what he had. He did not propose to *chivvy* the *volatile* Supervisor, Mr Dewar, because he envisaged using him at a later date in his grand design for the school. He moved Miss Chima to Standard Two so that continuity might be maintained in the Infant classes by keeping Mr Obiako there. Standard Two pupils jumped for joy.

The *innovation* of: "Better teaching without the cane" seemed to be taking root. It was hard-going for some at the beginning. Mr Agomuo, now the Standard Four teacher, found it hardest. He had everything against him. Standard Four at the best of times was the most difficult class to teach. He was taking over in the second term, but so were others. He had a stammer, not a bad one, but it could get bad when he was angry. Sometimes when he could not make headway with his teaching, he would forget momentarily and shake his fist at some blundering pupil. Then he would remember the new staff motto:

"Better teaching without the cane".

But, as time went on, even Mr Agomuo agreed that it seemed to be working. The pupils were less frightened of class work. They were beginning to think more clearly. They talked more freely but talked more sense. In the cane-happy days, some pupils deliberately chose the cane as the line of least re*sistance*. Instead of straining to think *under the shadow* of the cane, they were beaten and then were free until the next round of questions.

Now they were learning to think. They were beginning to feel that they let themselves down if they missed a sum or a spelling. Previously, it was the teacher they were letting down or so they felt.

Now pride in themselves was beginning to *creep in*. They were beginning to think, not for the teacher's benefit, but for their own. It was *remarkable*. Everyone was surprised and pleased, not least the pupils themselves. As a matter of fact, during the first week of term, they had thought they were enjoying the proverbial 'week of grace', but as time went on, they saw that the period of grace was becoming permanent. They did not need much persuasion to cooperate. After all, no one hankers after sore hands and backs.

Another early change inside the classroom was the introduction of the rotation of class monitors on a fortnightly basis in place of having one permanent, usually favoured and often *tyrannical,* monitor. This gave more pupils the chance to take responsibility. It also took the glamour out of being the 'teacher's stooge'.

Mr Obiako, the Church teacher, was acting as a wonderful link between Mr Mozie and the Committee of church elders. He was also showing Mr Mozie how to deal with the townspeople in general. The former Headmaster's letter through the Committee, thanking them for their big-hearted and open-handed send off and exhorting them to 'help the young Headmaster at least as much as you helped me', also did much to soften the feelings of the town people towards Mr Mozie. They had sent off the petition written for them by Stanislaus to the Reverend Mr Jones, but did not follow it further. They had already decided to leave matters as they were unless Mr Mozie *rubbed them up* the wrong way. So far he had not.

Mr Obiako was helping the Headmaster in his first major demand from the townspeople. Mr Mozie wanted land. Mr Obiako cautioned him that the demand should not be made with a direct confrontation. Asking these people for land was akin to asking them for their lives. It would be unwise to make a direct demand. In fact, if Mr Obiako had not believed very fervently in the Headmaster's quiet revolution, he would have advised against the project altogether, at least for a year or two. He agreed with the Headmaster that the school needed a good playing-field if they were ever to stop being the laughing-stock of the district in competitive sports. Mr Mozie's plan was to make a playing-field on the site of the school farm and he needed another piece of land for the school farm. He also proposed to convert part of the teacher's large back gardens into a smaller playing-field. He was determined that the children should have ample opportunity for developing their bodies as well as their minds.

He worked out with Mr Obiako the best way of presenting the request to the townspeople without stirring up their *antagonism*. They decided that the best move would be to invite some members of the Committee to accompany the school to the next Empire Day celebrations in Umuahia. Letting them see the poor showing of their school children in the athletic competition would be the surest way of bringing home to them the

need for a better playing field in the school.
After that, Mr Obiako suggested, their
resistance to improvements in the school would
be reduced.

4

Ceremony with Joyo

Empire Day, the twenty-fourth of May, was always a happy occasion for pupils all over the district. They all looked forward to it. At the Central School Amanzu the feeling was the same. They looked forward to marching to Umuahia. They did not have a full school band, but the side-drum, bugle, flute and cymbals which they had, were sufficient for their marching songs. They looked forward to the march past the saluting base where the District Officer stood in his gleaming white uniform and white helmet. They looked forward to the athletic competition which followed the popular police band, the bands from other schools, and the prize-giving in the afternoon, and the homecoming. It was always a jolly good outing. Missing school for a whole day was also not to be regretted.

When, therefore, the Headmaster announced that Empire day was on the following Thursday and that as usual the whole school would march to Umuahia for the celebrations, he was widely cheered by the whole school. From the sound of that ap*plause*, one would have thought that he was offering them something they had never had before. Perhaps missing Good Friday and Easter celebrations in school had heightened their *enthusiasm* for this other public celebration.

Everyone was on their best behaviour during the week before Empire Day. On the eve of the celebrations the school was closed so that each pupil could make sure of a neat uniform and a *decent* hair cut for the occasion.

The time for setting off, half past six, added to the excitement of the day. The Headmaster did not invite the selected Committee men to march with the school. Most of them had bicycles and he asked them to go to Umuahia when they wished, provided they were at the Rest House Field to watch the march past at nine.

The dawn assembly was more prompt than the usual assembly for school at eight o'clock. Only a very few *stragglers* joined the lines after school had marched out of the grounds. Two boys led the column carrying a large white placard bearing the name of the school. The other pupils were arranged according to height, with the tallest at the back. The band brought up the rear, while the teachers were spaced regularly down the line, walking beside the children. They were not armed with canes-not this term.

There was a *mammoth* crowd on the field at Umuahia. There were school children from various schools in their white tunics or shirts and white shorts. The schools were identified by large white placards held *aloft* by their standard-bearers. Girls from Roman Catholic schools wore royal-blue uniforms, and those from the convents had white dresses and headscarves.

There was the police band, which seemed to be *rehearsing* rather too loudly, and there were the barrel chested policemen in full parade kit. They wore black berets, black short-sleeved jumpers. Thickly-starched green khaki shorts, black woolen puttees and heavy shiny black boots rather than a wintery uniform for the tropics! Compared with the beefy Police contingent, the court Messengers, who were also uniformed and on parade, looked *scruffy* and underfed. They wore threadbare navy-blue tunics and shorts, caps to match, and black puttees, but no shoes. A handful of Boy Scouts in brown and Wolf Cubs in green darted around helping the policemen to organise the crowd.

The reserved seats were occupied by colourfully attired chiefs, in feathered hats or cloth caps, and the top civil servants and business men of the district. The crowd awaited the arrival of the District Officer, the only event which could be expected to quieten them. As the morning warmed up under a clear cloudless May sky, the multitude grew, and with it the noise.

The drill competition for schoolboys, which followed the march past, was conducted by a bull-voiced police officer. A trophy was awarded to the winning school, but there were no individual prizes. However, quite a few boys were known in the past to have been ear-marked for the police as a result of their performance in this contest.

Mr Mozie was sad but not surprised to see the Amanzu School squad eliminated early in the contest. He was standing and chatting with Mr Offor, who had brought his new school to the celebrations. Mr Mozie was neither surprised, nor sad, when Mr Offor's school squad was *eliminated* soon after.

Athletics proper followed the drill competition. The morning session produced no surprises for Mr Mozie, and no winners. His boys tried, but were outclassed. His girls did no better. His lone *consolation* came just before the lunch break, in the may-pole dance. This was the girls' special competition in place of the boys' drill contest. Central School Amanzu came third, thanks to the coaching which Miss Chima had given under the all-purpose mango trees back in the school compound.

As if to continue with lunch, the first athletic event after the long interval was the ever-popular 'Banana race' for the children from the infant classes. Everyone came back in time so as not to miss it.

The announcement was made that all the little children should come into the middle of the field for the event. This was repeated over and over again until all those who were qualified to take part in the *contest* were on field. Any of the bigger children who looked as if they might make it an unequal contest were sent off. The competitors were counted and then divided into three groups. A thick rope with half-peeled bananas suspended from it was run right across the field, twenty five yards from the starting line. The first group of competitors was lined up given the usual instructions by the starter: "I will say: 'Ready, steady, go!' And when you hear: 'Go! You run to the banana straight in front of you, and eat it without touching it with your hands. You must hold both hands behind your back. When you have finished eating, run back here as fast as you can. The first to get back here will be the winner. Do you all understand?"

There was a loud roar of: "Yes," accompanied by their head noddings. Even the other groups of competitors standing back joined in the chorus.

The first group ran the race of their lives to the banana line and then the fun started. With their hands behind their backs and the line jerking, it was a job to get more than a bite. Some children tried to steady the target with their shoulders. Others *threw caution and the rules* to *the wind,* and chewed through the banana skin to complete their *mission*. The most impatient took a mouthful and dashed back. But the judges at both ends were *vigilant*. Anyone who obviously did not do justice to his or her banana, or returned to the finishing line still *munching* a mouthful was disqualified. The judges managed to get three winners.

As the second group was being lined up for a race, a *chubby* little girl in a brown school dress *toddled* onto the field and calmly joined the third group. Some of the other children in that group tried to push her away, shouting:

"You were not counted! You're not with us."
The track steward ordered them to leave her
alone. "There are more than enough bananas for
everyone."

Meanwhile the first rope had been taken
away and a second one, sagging with fresh half-
peeled bananas, was run across the field.

After two false starts and a threat to send all
of them away, the second group went off to the
roar of the crowd, who were by now *closing in
on* the field to get a better view.

The chubby late entrant would not be
rushed. She went at her own pace, only a little
faster than when she came onto the field. The
crowd *reeled* with laughter. They had seen the
perfect loser. Some cheered. Others jeered.
Chubby-face raced on, straight ahead *in
complete obedience of* the starter's orders. By
the time she got to the banana line, most of her
rivals were on their way back. A few still
struggled with their unsteady targets. She

ignored them. The first and only thing to *ruffle* her that afternoon was the discovery that the banana she had been heading for had been eaten obviously, she thought, by someone who could not have known what a straight line meant. But she did not stand around and bemoan her fate. She just turned right and walked down the line, turning up banana skins until she found one which had not been eaten. She pulled it right off the line, peeled it neatly and completely, and began eating *with all the elegance of* a well-bred princess.

The *tumult* around the field was getting louder, Someone called: "Joy, what are you doing?", but the little girl heard nothing. When she had finished, she wiped her hands on her skirt, and as the deafening noise continued, she turned and walked up the banana line again, resuming her inspection. She rejected any half-eaten bananas, found only two more untouched ones, pulled them off, and was about to repeat her delicate peeling act when she heard her name above the noise: "Joy, run back!"

She recognized the voice, turned, and started on her way back to the finishing line, a banana in each hand.

Few people in the cloud saw who won the third race. Few cared. Every eye was on Joy.

......until she found one which had not been
eaten.

The crowd, hearing her name, took up the chant: "Joy, run back! Joy, run back!" She ran at her own pace, neither quickened nor slowed down by the chanting. Eventually she arrived. At the finishing line, she was picked up by a laughing Miss Chima while her embarrassed mother was threatening to *spank* her. Joy was one of Miss Chima's 'babies' and it was Miss Cima's call which had sent Joy running back. The laughter died down slowly.

The rest of the afternoon was taken up by other track and field events: sprints, sack races, obstacle races, a three legged race, the jumps (high, long and pole vault), and finally the relay races. There was also a tug-of-war between the police and a combined team of Boy Scouts and Court Messengers. But there was nothing *to touch* the *pleasure* of Joy's performance. She had stolen the afternoon. If not the whole day's show.

At the end of the day, there were trophies and prizes *galore,* which were presented by the District Officer's wife.

To Mr Mozie's disappointment but not surprise, pupils from the Central School Amanzu were called up only three times. First was for the third place in the girls' maypole dance, second for second place in the junior hundred yards, and third? Why! The third call was for Joy. The District Officer's wife had asked for a special prize for her, a tin of biscuits, for her performance in the banana race. When her name was called, the crowd led her up to receive her prize, she was applauded all the way there and back. Joy was her same chubby self, unruffled and unhurrying.

At the end of the day the pupils marched back to their respective schools, singing: "Gods save the King" and other songs. Between marching songs, the events of the day were discussed *animatedly*. Little quarrels resulted from disagreement over minor details, but these were quickly settled. The mood of Empire Day was too *buoyant* for serious quarrels.

A less light-hearted view of the results of the competition was held in other quarters. Earlier in the day, Matthew had gone over to greet Mr Offor who was chatting with Mr Mozie.

"Good morning, H.M. How is the family?" "Ah! My good friend. How are you? How is Martha, your good wife, and how are the children?" Mr Offor responded, stretching out his hands to take Matthew's.

"They are all very well, H.M. How is your new school?"

"Quite *good*. I am happy to be there. What brought you to these celebrations? You have never been here before?"

"You are quite right, H.M. I never thought it was a place for old men, but the new H.M. suggested that some of us should come to see what the school children do. Now I see that even older men from other places are here."

"And perhaps you have also seen what I told you about our own children's performance," Mr Mozie prompted.

"Indeed, I have, and I think something, ought to be done about it," Matthew responded.

"Well, I don't *envy* those schools which lay undue emphasis on athletics at the expense of school work and discipline," Mr Offor countered.

"Do you really believe improvement in athletic standards can harm class work or school discipline?" Mr Mozie asked.

"Achievements on the field often go to the athletes' heads and they begin to imagine that they are more important than other pupils," Mr Offor replied.

"Whatever it does to them, I would still have liked to see our children beating others on this field," Matthew said.

At this point, some other Committee men from Amanzu, who had seen Matthew standing with the two Headmasters, came to join them.

After they had exchanged greetings with Mr Offor, Matthew introduced them to the argument. Opinion was divided.

That was all Mr Mozie wanted. As the Committee men battled with the problem, he and Mr Offor left to attend to some official business with one of the other Headmasters.

Throughout the rest of the day and on the way home Matthew and his men *debated* the problem. On one point they were convinced by the evidence of their own eyes: that Central School Amanzu was one of the poorest schools on the sports field on that day.

Matthew did not let it rest at that, but brought the matter up formally at the full Committee meeting. From there the discussion spread to involve the whole community. The community was thus *alerted* to the problem and the stage was set for Mr Mozie's plan to ask for their support in providing better sports facilities for his school.

5

The Biggest Ally Visits Amanzu

Mr Mozie left Mr Biako to continue the *liaison* work with the Committee. Meanwhile, he decided to *consolidate the gains* made in the classrooms and to see what further improvements could be made. His only worries were the Standards Three and Four teachers, Mr Okehi and Mr Agomuo. These two were co-operating *in fits and starts;* but often seemed to be *making heavy weather of* teaching without the cane. This was reflected in the *comparatively* poor weekly text results from these two classes. He had also noticed that in the regular Staff Meetings he had introduced, these two teachers showed less keenness than the rest.

Happily, the majority were *pulling their weight*. Mr Ibe of Standard Five and Mr Obasi of Standard One both identified themselves with the dreams and with the effort required to realize them. As for Miss Chima, she was an angel. She was doing a great job in Standard Two and still finding time to help the Infant classes and to encourage the girls in the higher classes. He could not imagine what he would have done without her. He almost felt like rejoicing at the *partial* closure of her old school which led to Amanzu being blessed by her presence.

But Mr Mozie's greatest gratitude went to Mr Obiako for being so *young at* heart in spite of his age and lack of formal education. Mr Obiako's cooperation had far exceeded Mr Mozie's expectations. He was the most *ardent* believer in the Headmaster's programme; and,

Mr Mozie saw clearly, the key to any success he might achieve.

In the next Staff meeting, Mr Mozie raised the question of *stimulating* the competitive spirit in their pupils both inside and outside the classrooms. Mr Obiako suggested that end of term examination results should be called out in order of merit from the first to the last person.

"This," he said, "will put into the pupils' heads the idea of striving to improve their positions if they are poor. It doesn't matter if those at the top boast. The shame will be theirs when they go down and others up. We used to do this before, you know, but ... it was changed, and the 'Pass or Fail' method introduced."

Various ideas were discussed, from calling the results out in the individual classes, to calling them out in public gathering, to writing them out on blackboards, to sending them home to the parents. The final decision was that individual classrooms were the best place.

Public display or calling out the result would lead to *cheeky* children in the lower classes teasing senior pupils in the higher classes who were at the bottom of their class. However, the idea of a public announcement was agreed to when Mr Ibe *modified* it. The names of the top three pupils in each class would be called out during the final Assembly at the end of the term. Someone slipped in the ideas of giving prizes of books or stationery to these pupils.

Then Miss Chima suggested a competition in written and spoken English. Developing her *theme*, she suggested that the competition could be arranged in two groups, senior and junior, for the classes (Standards one to Six) which learned English. Up to that point, the other teachers were with her, or at least they listened patiently. Then she spoiled her case by adding that there had been such a competition in the Girls' Demonstration School.

Mr Agomou growled: "We want original ideas and not those borrowed wholesale from another school. We don't want to be a carbon copy of Miss Hill's school."

The Headmaster was glad to see Mr Agomuo take an interest in the discussion even if he was rude and his interest was negative.

Mr Obiako turned to Mr Agomuo: "No idea is new under the sun. Anything you may say or do has been said or done before. So, whether an idea comes from a girls' school or from a market, all we want to see is if it can help our children here."

The suggestion was discussed fully. A compromise solution was found. English was too narrow a theme for such a competition. General knowledge was substituted, but it was not going to be the dull unimaginative type of test they had in the past. They would *devise* questions to stimulate the children's creative imagination. Miss Chima was satisfied and so were the others. As for the Headmaster, he knew that this was progress.

Mr Dewar, the Supervisor of school, was due to visit the school on the following Wednesday, his first visit since Mr Mozie had taken over. The usual *flurry* of activity in preparation for the Supervisor's visit went on throughout the preceding week and into the week of the visit. The classroom benches and desks were scrubbed and polished. The blackboards were blackened, the doors and windows cleaned and the walls and ceilings given a thorough dusting. Outside, the walls of the buildings, the Assembly Square and the playground, the teachers' garden and the handwork shcd all got extra attention. Finally, the hedges, the gates, the school farm and the grey weather-cock on the Assembly Hall all got a good going over. The school was ready.

Mr Dewar could never arrive quietly, let alone secretly. His heavy motorbike could be heard over a mile away. The hand bell had gone for change of lessons when the first sound of his noisy machine was heard in the distance. Within minutes, however, he had bumped his way past the town into the school, hailed and greeted all the way by groups of people on their way to the market or to the farms. A number of excited children *trailed* him, through the fumes he left and dust he raised, to the school. They arrived at the gate, surprisingly, not long after

"*You seem to be* getting on *well with your* new
job, Joseph."

him. They must have been running hard.

Mr Mozie was at the south gate to receive the Supervisor and to wheel the heavy machine into the shade of his own front verandah. Mr Dewar brushed back his *dishevelled* hair with his hands and combed out his reddish-brown beard with his fingers. The inspection began.

They went from one classroom to the other, and in each were received with the customary: "Class up!... Salute!... Class sit!" Mr Dewar watched the lesson in each class for some minutes, and then moved on. The Headmaster's instructions had been that each teacher was to go on with the ordinary lessons in the usual way. There were to be no *embellishments* and no specially prepared lessons.

Mr Dewar made no comments. When they finished with the classrooms, they went to the Headmaster's office for Mr Dewar's inspection of the registers, the accounts books, the monthly and quarterly returns, and the files.

Then Mr Mozie took the Supervisor round the school premises and to the school farm. As they walked along Mr Dewar said: "You seem to be getting on well with your new job, Joseph."

"Thank you, sir, we are trying to do the work as a team, and my colleagues are all doing their best for the children." "Tell me, was this classroom show of teaching without the cane put on my benefit, or have all your pupils suddenly become geniuses?"

"No, sir. We did not do it as a show. It is an experiment we have been trying out, to see what effect it would have on the children's interest and their *appreciation* of the lessons we teach them. We thought it might be possible that the cane hindered rather than helped the children."

"And where did you copy the idea from or perhaps you read it in a book?"

"We developed the idea here."

"Hm-m-m. I see. Any results?"

"So far, quite encouraging. The children certainly seem to be more alert; less frightened, and more *responsive*. They are generally keener on school work."

"Very well. And your teachers?"

"They all seem to be enjoying their work more."

"All of them?"

"They are all doing their best."

"And your little lady teacher. How is she doing here?"

"She does her best like the rest."

"Your Standard Four teacher seemed to be making heavy of it."

"Oh, Mr Agomuo stammers, That is his chief difficulty"

"I see. Well, Joseph, whoever or whatever gave you the idea that you could teach in this part of the world without the cane, I must say I wish you luck. You'll tell me later the final results of your experiment. Your farm looks rich. What have you got in it?"

Mr Mozie went through the list of crops in the farm. The Supervisor knew something about yams. They inspected the compost pit in the middle of the farm, and were on their way back to the school when the Supervisor gave Mr Mozie the lead he had been praying for.

"No experiments on the farming side yet, like farming without the hoe?" Mr Dewar asked, teasingly.

"Oh no, not yet. I had *toyed* with the idea of making a playing field on this farm site but..."

"I thought as much," Mr Dewar broke in. "You don't believe in half measures, do you?"

"Far from it. I would prefer a bigger and better school farm if I could get another suitable piece of land. As you can see, we have no real playing-field in this school. Our poor showing in sports stems from this lack."

Mr Dewar listened as the Headmaster unfolded his plan for developing recreational facilities in the school, but made no comment.

As they approached the playground behind the main block, Mr Dewar remembered the little girl who had caused the sensation in the banana race on Empire Day, and asked the Headmaster about her.

"Oh, that's little Joy Amadi."

"Yes, indeed. Joy was her name," Mr Dewar remembered. "I've got a little present for her. Where can we see her?"

That's very kind of you. We should find her in the playground. She will be delighted."

The pupils had obeyed the Headmaster's instructions that they should spend their recess as usual and not mill around the Supervisor as though he had come to entertain the school. The playground was therefore full when the Supervisor and Mr Mozie arrived there. Unfortunately, they could not find Joy. They were told that she had not come to school that morning because her mother was ill.

Mr Dewar spoke a few words of Ibo to some of the children. They were *thrilled,* and not to be outdone, they spoke to him in English.

One said: "Sir, visit Joy at home."

Mr Dewar asked the Headmaster if this was possible. Mr Mozie said that it was easy since the little girl lived near the school. Miss Chima offered to accompany them. Mr Dewar took a parcel out of a bag on his motorcycle and they set out.

As they approached the house, Joy saw them and began chanting happily: "Miss is coming." Then less enthusiastically, she announced: "The Headmaster is coming with Miss." She ran out to meet her friend Miss Chima.

Joy's mother was worried to hear that the Headmaster was coming to her home. She hoped he was not furious with her for not sending Joy to school. She got up, picked up her walking stick, and was walking out to meet her visitors on the verandah when Joy came back with Miss Chima in *tow*. Miss Chima greeted her and asked her how she was getting on. "A little better than you, Miss," she replied. "This leg still feels like *a log of wood.*"

When Miss Chima told her that the Supervisor of Schools had come with the Headmaster to see her little girl, Mrs Amadi was really alarmed. "Good Lord, Why? What can

I offer them to eat?"

"Don't worry about that. They have only come to say hello to Joy," Miss Chima reassured her.

Mr Dewar greeted Mrs Amadi to put her at ease.

"Good morning, Mrs Amadi."

"Good morning, sir," Mrs Amadi replied. "Please sit down. I hope nothing is wrong. Is it my little girl, Joy? What can I offer you? What can I offer them Miss? My husband has gone to the shop, he would have known what to offer..."

Mr Mozie stepped in to help her out of her anxiety. "Please don't brother yourself, Mrs Amadi. We have only come to say hello to little Joy. We are sorry to see that you are ill, and hope you soon get better, The Supervisor remembered little Joy from Empire Day

Mrs Amadi covered her face. Joy smiled and did not cover her face.

"The Supervisor has brought little Joy a present," the Headmaster continued.

Mr Dewar smiled and stroked his beard. He handed a packet of biscuits to Joy, who was still *clutching* Miss Chima's hand.

"Won't you thank him, Joy?" Her mother urged even before the child had taken hold of the packet,

"Sir, thank you," Joy said, curtsying neatly.

Her mother thanked Mr Dewar again and pressed her visitor to sit down. "Our custom forbids us to let a visitor go without sitting down first, even if briefly. He need not take food or drink, but he must not *spurn* the hospitality of our chair," she explained.

The visitors asked Mrs Amadi about her illness and were assured that she was recovering. Unnoticed by them, she had signalled instructions to her house-maid, who had been peeping through the doorway. So, as they rose to leave after wishing her a speedy recovery, the maid came out with three parcels, one for each of them.

Mrs Amadi asked if they wanted to take Joy back to the school with them. Miss Chima asked her if she wanted to go.

"Yes, Miss, I want to come," cried Joy.

"Come along then, " Mr Dewar called, laughing.

Back in the school, Mr Dewar thanked Miss Chima for her help. As Miss Chima returned to the classroom with little Joy, Mr Dewar went back with the Headmaster to his house. It was only then Mr Mozie discovered that he had, that day, met his biggest ally.

Mr Dewar promised to send Mr Mozie a new teacher but added that he could only spare an untrained teacher. He also promised to secure a grant, however small, from the Manager, Reverend Mr Jones, for the preparation of the playing-field. He expressed enthusiasm for Mr Mozie's plans to reform the school but cautioned him not to push the people of Amanzu too fast. From experience, he knew that village people are suspicious of rapid change, and that although they would support him while things went well they would withdraw their support and turn against him in the event of any failure. He must therefore try to obtain their agreement by explaining each plan patiently.

6

New Ideas in Practice

The effect of the ceremony of calling up the top three pupils in each class at the end of the term to receive prizes from the Headmaster was remarkable. The pupils were warmly applauded, like prize winners in athletics. It was the first public *acclaim* for achievement in school work.

The third term started with one noticeable feature: eagerness. The school children certainly looked eager, and the teachers seemed to find more joy in teaching. Even the two reluctant ones, Mr Agomuo and Mr Okehi, seemed to feel guilty about letting the side down with poor examination results at the end of the second term. Mr Dewar had sent the promised junior teacher, Mr Etim.

Emboldened by Mr Dewar's support, and aided by Mr Obiako's liaison and *subtle propaganda,* Mr Mozie launched his daring playing-field plan. He met little difficulty. The Church committee saw the village head, and secured a plot of land on the east side of the school compound beyond the old trade route. They also promised to help with the heavier work in making the field. They would organize *relays* of such men to work two days in the week until the field was ready for the planting of Bahama grass, which the school children could do.

The teachers willingly gave up part of their back gardens as soon as the crops had been harvested. The Headmaster proposed that the school should be entirely responsible for making the smaller field on this site. It would give the children a sense of achievement, and help them appreciate the great contribution the Committee was making in undertaking the work on the bigger field.

He reported his success to Mr Dewar who followed it up by writing to the Reverend Mr Jones a grant of five pounds towards the construction of the playing field. This small sum did not dismay Mr Mozie. No labour costs would be involved, and he could get one of the carpenters in the Church to make the goal-posts at little cost. The rest of the money would be spent by Matthew for feeding the voluntary workers on the days they worked.

Mr Mozie did not allow himself to *be carried away* from the work in the classrooms.

All the points raised in his *predecessor's* farewell speech were still in his head and, until he had dealt with each one of them, he was not satisfied. He thought he would deal next with the school's *lamentable* singing record.

Mr Brown-Wilcox, the West African Trading Company Assistant Manager, was a great music lover. That point must have escaped Mr Offor, to whose wife Mr Brown-Wilcox was distantly related. Mr Brown-Wilcox owned a large upright piano and gave concerts and lessons to people in the town. When Mr Mozie approached him, he had no hesitation in accepting the job of official but unpaid music master. To him music was next to a religion, and in his own words, he: "Jumped at any opportunity to make *converts*".

But when he began his music lessons, his enthusiasm was nearly killed by what he saw, or rather, heard from the pupils of the Central School. Any but the most dedicated teacher would have given up. Perhaps he exaggerated, but the standard was decidedly poor. He gave lessons in the school in the evening and took smaller groups home for more lessons around the piano. The charm of the piano music undoubtedly helped to *kin*dle their interest. They made sufficient progress for him to form a good school choir from the most promising ones.

How to help school-leavers was the Headmaster's next concern. There were few secondary schools and they were difficult to get into. The best known in the Eastern Provinces at that time was the Hope Waddell Training Institute in Calabar, but Mr Mozie realized that getting any pupils into that great institution called for more than dreaming. Besides, the Institute was expensive. The few Government Colleges in other parts of the country offered scholarships, but it would be some time before he could consider those within the reach of even his best pupils. But he decided that he must try to do something about this.

He conferred with the teachers on a coaching programme for the pupils in Standard four and five with next year's entrance examinations in view. Of those in Standard *Six*, only two had put in for an entrance examination and they were already being coached. The rest needed to be guided into good jobs or training schools. The Headmaster *combed* the country for training facilities not previously *revealed* to the pupils, and assured parents that their children would not be ruined morally if they went far away to train at Lagos or Kaduna or Enugu where the Civil Service Training Schools were situated. He determined that his pupils should *venture further afield* instead of walking tamely into local jobs.

As the third term was rolling to its close, the school seemed to be approaching the shape which Mr Mozie *envisaged.* The cane as an instrument of classroom instruction had become a thing of the past. The pupils were working with visible enthusiasm towards their final examinations and General Knowledge competition. Absenteeism and truancy were on the *wane*. Matthew was proving himself a tireless foreman of works in the construction of the new playing-field. His enthusiasm was infectious. Even the schoolchildren, hard-pressed by impending school examinations and by work on the smaller field, found time to help the volunteers. Mr Brown-Wilcox had formed a school choir whose impact on Sunday services had become noticeable.

With all these achievements most people would probably have been content to relax until the end of the year. Mr Mozie had other ideas. He felt that relaxing equaled idling. So he turned his attention to the new young teacher, Mr Etim.

Mr Etim came from Calabar province, but his mother was Ibo and he spent his early childhood in Abiriba, his mother's hometown. He had later gone to school in Calabar and had been teaching in a smaller village school near Umuahia before he was transferred to Amanzu.

He was working as a pupil teacher while awaiting an opportunity to go to a Teacher Training College.

Mr Etim felt quickly at home in Amanzu. The Headmaster gave him the spare room in his own house, which Miss Chima had occupied when she lived with the Offors.

What attracted the Headmaster's attention to the new teacher was his great interest in Scouting. Mr Etim had been a Wolf Cub and then a Boy Scout in Calabar. There were no Scouts or Cubs in Amanzu. Since his arrival, Mr Etim had spent every Tuesday afternoon in the same way he had done for years-Scouting. Immediately after the afternoon school session, he would return to his room, dress up in his full Scout uniform and go up to the hill to practice *signalling* or revise his Morse code or practice tying knots.

***Mr* Etim practising signalling.**

At other times, he would go to the bush and practice climbing or making track signs. Occasionally he would jog round the school compound a few times and then go into the village to help out someone with one odd job or the other.

Mr Mozie was not the only person interested in Mr Etim's activities on Tuesday afternoons. Some of the pupils *plied* Mr Etim with questions about the Scout movement. "Is it a religious movement?" "Does it have anything to do with the Salvation Army?" "Is it a secret society?" "Was the movement started in Calabar?" "Could it help anyone get into the Police or into other jobs?" Is it expensive to join?".

When Mr Etim told them the story of Baden-Powell and how simple the aims of the movement were, they were even more interested. He talked to them about the development of their bodies and minds, about character building, about leadership training and about helping people in trouble. When, however, he turned to joys of hiking, camping, swimming, helping at football matches and

Empire Day celebrations and sending of messages by signalling, they all wanted to become Scouts

The Headmaster was prepared to encourage Scouting in the school. First he got Mr Etim's agreement and Mr Dewar's approval. Then a Staff Meeting agreed that a Wolf Cub pack would be best for a start, with a Scout troop later if the Wolf Cubs were a success.

7

Harmattan Takes a Hand

A worse day could not have been chosen for the reopening of school in the New Year. **It** was the third week in January. The country **was** in the grip *of* its driest and dustiest harmattan for years. It had for years. It had started around Christmas, and at that festive time the **first** few days were quite tolerable, in fact enjoyable. There were open-air fires for the cold mornings, unbroken sunshine *without* a *whiff of* cloud in the sky for the day-long dancing and merriment, and cool moonlit nights for the communal story-telling or, for the young ones, games by moonlight in the village squares.

But, as the days passed, the harmattan became *uncomfortable*. The land was parched;

rivulets and wells dried up; the air became thin. When the wind blew it raised *swirls* of dust which came near to blinding the people. Dry skin and cracked lips became common complaints. To a people noted for their hearty boisterous laughter, these were a grave handicap. Talk and laughter became rather subdued for fear of widening t cracks on the lips, and this led to the popular joke among children: "You are talking and laughing like a European. What's happened to your mouth?"

It was in this climate that school reassembled. One thing was immediately obvious, the harmattan might have dried up the land, the wells, the rivulets and the vegetation, but it had not dried up the children's enthusiasm. On the first day of term, attendance was excellent. There were new pupils from other schools seeking admission into every class; but the most numerous and most entertaining of the new pupils were those in

Infant One. There were rows and rows of them standing with their mothers around the vestry end of the Assembly Hall. In those days there were no birth certificates, and therefore no reliable way of deciding who had reached the official school age of six years. In every school, the traditional yard stick of having reached school age was the ability of the child to put one arm over the top of his head to touch the opposite ear with the fingertips. Mr Mozie, with all his ingenuity and his flair for change, had not found a substitute for it.

As the young children stood there that morning waiting to be examined and hoping to be enrolled after morning prayers, many of the smaller ones could be seen practising. They stretched and strained their ears, while their mothers helped by pulling and tugging at the tiny arms to get the maximum stretch out of them. What devices did they not get up to in order to improve their dear one's chances?

Some poor children had their heads shaved clean and oiled so that they could gain easier access across the top. They were taught to retract their necks (tortoise fashioning) while stretching their arms to touch their ears, and to shrug the appropriate shoulder if that would help. If the mothers could have re-moulded those little heads without hurting their children, they would have done so. Getting into school was so important and yet so difficult, and many of the children were clearly under age.

Apart from the new pupils and the absence of the previous year's Standard Six, Central School Amanzu was pretty well the same. There had been only one change in the staff. Mr Okehi had been transferred to another school and a Mr Eze had come to take his place.

As usual, every staff movement provoked *rumours* and raised questions. Did Mr Mozie ask for Mr Okehi's transfer because of his friendship with the former Headmaster? Was it a move to break the Agomuo-Okehi *axis* which has become visibly *obdurate* in Staff Meetings and a drawback to the entire programme of progress? Had Mr Okehi's poor examination results led to his transfer? But Mr Agomuo's result had been no better, so there was no certainty that this had had anything to do with the transfer. Or, was it only a routine transfer with no ulterior motive.

The greatest problem which the harmattan had set the school was in the playing fields. The Headmaster talked at length in his opening speech about the debt of gratitude the whole school owed to the townspeople, under the leadership of the Committee, for their work on the field during the Christmas holidays. Then he added that until grass grew on the fields, they could not really be called fields.

During recess, there was a *stampede* to go and have another look at the large field. s and the ropes were still there, but *to all* intents and *purposes*, the work had been completed. But the scorched Bahama grass which had been planted when the workers levelled the field was a depressing sight. The grass would have to be planted all over again, but for the moment the land at woh las was too parched for that.

Everyone who saw the bare dusty fields felt concerned. The pupils discussed the problem animatedly. There were as many suggestions as there were onlookers. The Headmaster had forbidden any playing or running on the fields until they were ready. That meant waiting for many months for the rainy season to arrive to help the grass to grow, unless something could be done about it.

"The main trouble *is* water," someone said.

"Yes, yes, water is the trouble," others

"How can we get water to make the grass grow?"

"Oh, why not wait until the rainy season?

It is only four to five months more, isn't it?" a voice asked,

"Shut up, lazy fool, shut up!"

"All right, strong ones, let us divert the Ilo River through the field to water it? The lazy one retorted.

This led to hilarious laughter among some of his opponents and seething anger among others.

"Who's the lazy drone who doesn't want to water the field?" one bully asked.

"And who's the rain doctor who wants to call down the rain?" the lazy one taunted. There was more laughter.

The bully elbowed his way through the throng towards the lazy one shouting: "Who did you call the rain doctor?"

"And who did you call lazy drone?"

As the rest of the crowd drew back to watch the opening battle of the year, the bully flashed out a full-blooded backhand slap which caught the opponent (Frederick Osiogu, now a Standard Three pupil) on the right cheek. This was more than anyone could take. As the bully stretched his hand to grip his tunic, Frederick dived and caught him by the ankles. Frederick then tried to stand up with the bully over his back, but the bully clutched his shorts and would not let go. They cart-wheeled into the smaller field and were soon lost in a cloud of sand and dust.

The other pupils cheered and jeered, while someone ran off to report to the nearest teacher, screaming as he ran: "Two fighting, sir!"

Mr Agomuo came along with the proud reporter, and at his approach, most of the pupils melted away, leaving a few keen onlookers to give their contrasting versions of the discussion which led up to the fight. Meanwhile the bully and Frederick had parted. It was impossible to say who was the winner. Each was a sorry brown mess.

Mr Mozie picked up ideas from the most unlikely circumstances. While examining the case of the two boys who had given such a wretched start to the term, and ordering the appropriate punishment to add to the bruises they had already inflicted on each other, one of their taunting phrases: 'diverting the river', struck him. He decided that he had to "divert" the river on the heads and shoulders of the pupils. As the townspeople had given so much in sweat and toil, he must try something drastic to save the fields.

He ordered general *mobilization* for the campaign of grassing both fields by the end of the term. The streams had not dried up, and two buckets of water a day for each pupil during the week, and two buckets on Saturday morning should be enough to water the fields. He girdled the fields with large barrels borrowed from the commercial house in town. These served as reservoirs for the water. Then he ordered crude watering cans from a parent who was a tinker. Until the farming started in earnest, he reckoned the pupils could concentrate on the fields. This water campaign was not allowed to disturb the classes, but fetching water for the teachers was suspended.

The grounds of the old Rest House supplied all the Bahama grass that was needed to replant the field. The grass had been planted by prisoners who, having little to do, extended the planting into the valley at the rear of the Rest House. This valley, wooded and further shaded by a large banana grove, still grew beautiful, rich grass, green and easy to dig up, even with the dry season so severe.

At the best of times, grassing a field demands *meticulous* care in spacing *alignment* and depth of planting of the grass tufts. In the dry season it is doubly difficult. But the sense of mission with which staff and students alike faced the task made success inevitable. For a change, even Mr Agomuo worked his heart out on this project. His interest in football was probably an additional, if not the principal, driving force.

The weather nearly broke Mr Mozie and his gallant workers. The harmattan did not *relent*. It lasted well into February, and the drought continued until April. The parched earth absorbed all the water which was poured onto it. The first few batches of Bahama grass would not take root. If the Church Committee had not stepped in to help out once more, it would have been disastrous. As it was, good old Matthew rounded up his men again and they organized the women and girls and other children who did not go to school, to help. They brought water. Those who lived near the streams drew water from the streams. Others, to whom the springs were more accessible, went to these even though the springs were slowing down. By enlarging the crevices through which the water ran out of the rocks, and by fitting tin-E foil gutters or rolled up leaves into these *crevices* to prevent the water running down the sides of the rocks, enough water was trapped to make the trips worthwhile.

The water came. The water carriers dispensed *with the finesse* of the watering cans and soaked the fields all over. It worked. It was heart-warming to see the grass take root and grow. The brown rectangles were becoming green fields. Mr Mozie joyfully hoisted the goal-posts as a mark of progress and symbol of hope.

8

"Akela, We'll Do Our Best"

The Wolf Cub pack benefited from the help of the Church Committee in the grassing of the playing-fields. In the earlier back-breaking days of the 'water campaign' it was impossible *to contemplate* launching any new projects. But as relief came, the Headmaster gave Mr Etim the go-ahead, and made the announcement himself about the formation of the new group. He stressed that far from being another form of amusement and *frivolity*, being a Wolf Cub called for hard work and sacrifice rather than chean wards. He therefore did not want everyone to rush into joining. He indicated that as some of the activities would be unsuitable for the very young children, only those from

107

Standard Two upwards could join. Finally, he announced that all those boys who proposed to join should meet in the Assembly Hall after school on Tuesday.

In spite of the *austere* picture which the Headmaster had striven to paint in order to put off the lazy ones, Mr Etim had a good turn-out on Tuesday afternoon. He walked into the hall wearing his full scout uniform. He mounted the platform (on which the pulpit stood on Sundays) and gave his audience the two finger V-salute. This *startled* them and sent a *twitter* through the room. They did not understand his V-salute which resemble a gesture which in that part of the country was regarded as a curse meaning 'may you have twins'..

His first words to them were: "Wolf Cubs never live indoors, so all who *aspire* to become Wolf Cubs must follow me to the place where Wolf Cubs live." With that, he strode out of the room. The puzzled pupils ran after him.

He led them to the rough triangular clearing beyond the South Gate of the school. There he made them sit on the ground or on tree stumps or logs of wood. Then he began to tell them formally the stories some of them had heard from him in *bits and pieces*. He told them about Baden-powell, the founder of the Boy Scouts' Association, and how the movement had spread all over the world; then about the training for leadership, and about the roles of Boy Scouts and Wolf Cub in society. He threw in stories of heroic achievement of boy scouts and wolf cubs. Lastly, he told them about their own movement, the Wolf Cub movement; its history, its aims, its achievements, He repeated that Wolf Cubs lived out-of-doors and not indoors, in the woods rather than in classrooms. Then he went on: "From now on as Wolf Cubs, you will lead hard but free lives in the open, in the woods, on the hills, in the treetops, in the valleys and in the rivers."

The boys clapped though no one knew quite why. After the subsequent chattering subsided, Mr Etim continued: "For this first meeting, I shall teach you the first four simple things you must know as Wolf Cubs. All ready?"

"Yes, Sir!" they answered.

"First, the motto. It is the same for Wolf Cubs as for Boy Scouts, and is: 'be Prepared'. It is shortened to: 'B.P.' which you can see on the metal badge on my hat. It means what it says, that you must always be ready."

He made them repeat the motto a number of times. "The second thing to remember is the Wolf Cub promise: 'I promise to do my best, to do my duty to God and the King, to keep the rules of the Wolf Cub Pack, and to do a good turn to someone every day."

After they had *laboured* through that, phrase by phrase, he went on: "The third thing is the salute."

He *demonstrated* the V-sign with the index and the middle finger of the right hand held beside the right ear and facing forward with the remaining fingers held together. He explained first what the sign was not. "It was not the Twins curse". This sent a *ripple of laughter* through the group. The sign, he explained, represented the two ears of the Wolf Cub, and also signified the promises.

The facial and neck contortions which some of the boys went through in learning that simple salute needed to be seen to be believed.

Finally, Mr Etim introduced what he called the: *'Vow'*, which the whole troop must make anew to him at the beginning of each meeting. He told them that they would call him Akela, and the vow would be: "Akela, we'll do our best". Following that he would *enjoin* them four times to do their best, an order which would be abbreviated to: "D-Y. B! D-Y-B! D-Y-B! D-Y-B!" (Do Your Best!).

They would then make their final *affirmation:* "We'll do our best," abbreviated again to: "We'll D-O-B! D-O-B! D-O-B! D-O-B! (Do Our Best)."

After a few rehearsals, Mr Etim announced that the next meeting would be at the same time on the following Tuesday when they would be organized into groups, and uniforms, books and equipment would be discussed. He gave them the salute to which many responded, and then strode away, twigs and leaves cracking under his feet.

During the rest of the week the air rang with the magic words of the Wolf Cubs' motto, 'promise and vow'. Some boys teased their friends with them, saying them with *an* air *of mystery*. This made those who had not attended the first meeting jealous. Even the townsfolk were molested with those strange phrases, surely a misuse of the promise and a violation of the principles!

When Mr Etim arrived at the meeting the following week, he found a bigger crowd and he knew why. He gave them the salute to which they responded uncertainly.

Then he asked: "What is the Wolf Cub motto?"

"Be prepared," they shouted.

"Very *good*. Now then are you prepared?" "Yes, Sir!"

Mr Etim set them an impromptu test on what he had taught the previous week. He selected the best six for special coaching as potential leaders. He divided the remainder into groups of six.

"You do not become Wolf Cubs until you have received your caps," he explained, "and you cannot receive your caps until you have passed your first test. There will be rejections all along the line. Being a Wolf Cub is not easy. Only the best can succeed. I intend to start with only twenty-four Wolf Cubs this term, so *buckle your belts* and be prepared!" The movement was under way.

9

"No Bones, No Blood, No Entrails"

The *interminable* dry season ended *abruptly*. It was Good Friday. A *larger-than*-life "Ju-das" had been having his annual mauling. The heavens seemed to break loose. Following a sudden wind, it clouded over quickly, lightning flashed, thunder rumble, and down the rain came in sheets. There had been only two light drizzles in the preceding fortnight, scarcely a recognizable herald of this downpour which seemed more appropriate for August than for April.

After this freak beginning, the weather appeared to lose its bearing completely, for it continued to rain heavily as though in midseason. Easter was a washout. The week after, two heavy downpours threatened to wash the large playing field clear of all grass. Mr Mozie had *to* mount an immediate field-saving campaign, consisting of the building of a long gutter with feeder tracks on the north side of the field, and across the field to divert the floods. He had to squeeze this campaign into examination week, for it had to be done quickly if they were to avoid the prospect of returning after the holidays, to find the playing-fields bare once more.

The freak thunderstorms went as they came, without much *ceremony*, and the weather settled down to the normal *transi*tion from dry to wet during the month of May.

The second term saw the field bloom into a beautiful carpet-like green. The fence on the north side of the field was moved back to make room for a spectator's stand. The field * was soon put into use, unofficially until the *ceremonial* opening. Physical training was the first activity to be shifted from the Assembly Square to the new field. Then football practices were held under the supervision of Mr Agomuo, whose interest in the school as a whole seemed to have grown remarkably once the playing-field was in use. The new teacher, Mr Eze, was also keen on football and assisted Mr Agomuo with the coaching.

The official opening was fixed for the eve of the half-term holidays. A football match against the neighbour St. Luke's School was *scheduled* for this opening. The Headmaster 'extended invitations to the prominent people in town and to a few others from outside. Mr Dewar, the Supervisor, invited to kick-off and the W.A.T.C. Manager agreed to referee the match. Both Rend Father O'shea and Dr. Bankole-Eight from Umuahia also accepted the invasion, as did Mr Offor, the former Headmaster.

Mr Etim prepared his *fledgling* Wolf Cubs for their first appearance in public, while Mr Agomuo worked like *a beaver* to prepare the School XI. Mr Agomuo knew he had to make his team win their first match on their brand new field. They had never beaten St. Luke, but he believed that was because they had never had a good field to practise on. Mr Eze assisted Mr Agomuo, and the boys responded well.

Then Mr Agomuo suddenly fell ill. He complained of a high fever, *incessant* headaches, and, worst of all, bad dreams. When he failed to respond to quinine and other medicines from the Dispenser in the near-by Mission dispensary, he tried steam inhalations of boiled lemon grass and other aromatic leaves. Still he did not get better. He missed school, and more important to him, he missed the football coaching. Mr Eze had to take over.

Mr Agomuo began to be afraid: "Is this an ordinary illness?" He wondered. He could not think of anyone he had quarrelled with recently. "It couldn't be the football match?" But, nonsense, he was not going to play in the match, so why should anyone be after him? "It couldn't be," he thought. He kept turning over these questions in his mind.

One morning Stanislaus, the letter-writer, turned up to *sympathize* with him.

"Sorry to hear you're ill, B.M." Stanislaus greeted him. "Hello, Stan, how are you?"

Very well, thanks. Business is drying up, otherwise everything's okay." Then Stanislaus added: "1 hear you are coaching your boys for this great match. How's it going?" "Not well. It's these bad dreams. I can't sleep," Mr Agomuo answered.

"Dreams, did you say? I asked you about the coaching. But, tell me, who do you see in these bad dreams?

"Oh, no one in particular. Why?"

Well, I just wondered. You've heard of these people who trouble others in their dreams. There may be someone who's got something against you and "

"Nonsense! I don't believe in such things. Do you Stan?"

"Well, not really, but ...

"But what?" Mr Agomuo insisted.

"Oh, nothing. Have you heard from Mr Okehi recently... you know, your friend was transferred from here?"

"Frankly no, not since I replied to his first letter last term. But why do you ask?" ta "Have you dreamt about him lately?"

Stanislaus asked.

"As a matter of fact, I have. But that's nothing strange. We had had so many ex*ploits* together that there's nothing odd about him appearing in my dreams recently?"

"Why do you want to know, Stan? Do you interpret dreams?"

"No, but what was your so-called friend doing in your dreams? Did you see his face? Was his back not turned to you, and was he not trying *to bar* your way?"

Mr Agomuo did not answer. He was thinking. It was true he had not seen, Mr Okehi's face in his dreams. Stanislaus broke into his thoughts.

"Well, I suppose you have not heard of the saying 'friends today and enemies tomorrow', When I first heard that your so-called friend was grumbling that you *betrayed* him to the Headmaster and thereby caused his transfer, I didn't believe it. Later, however, I learnt on good authority that he had taken a vow to get at this school, dead or alive. You know where he comes from, don't you? There, they don't believe in half-measures."

Fear gripped Mr Agomuo. In his present state, he could not reason much, and was very suggestible. Stanislaus sensed this and exploited it.

"You must do something about it, B.M. I could see someone for you, someone who could save your life. He does not charge very much. The good ones never do." Stanislaus went on and on until, as often happened, he overplayed hand.

Suddenly Agomuo recovered his confusion and suggestibility, and resisted Stanislaus.

"No thank you Stan," he said boldly. "I don't believe in these things. No one is after me. It is a natural illness and I will get better."

"Very well then, if that's the way you feel about it. Goodbye," Stanislaus said. He got up and left.

The eve of the half-term holiday arrived. Mr Agomuo had still not recovered but he dragged himself on his *wobbly* legs to watch the match for which he had laboured to prepare his boys. He felt sure that fate had conspired to render him unfit to enjoy the match fully.

Everyone who had been invited attended, and a large crowd turned up to watch the match. Matthew, the Committee leader, was among the proudest and happiest people on the field. The Headmaster rightly gave him a place of honour among the distinguished guests.

Before the kick-off, the Catechist led the gathering in prayer and blessed the field, those who had worked on it, and those who would play on it. He prayed specially: "That this playing field should never see broken bones or blood or *entrails*, but only good games and goals."

The Catechist's prayers were *answered in full* that afternoon. Mr Dewar took the kickoff, and a goal feast followed. In their sparkling new red and white striped jerseys which the Headmaster, Mr Mozie, had introduced, the home team outshone and seemed to outnumber the St Luke's team who were playing in plain white vests. In the end the home team won 7-4, a goal tally which was inflated by an unbelievable number of penalties awarded by the referee, who would not allow any foul play.

For Mr Mozie the victory was not in beating St Luke's, but in being able to stage the match at all, on the sort of field he had dreamt about for so long.

Poor Mr Agomuo continued to feel poorly." Even the gratification of his team winning a football match was not enough to cure him. He spoke to the Headmaster about the visit he had had from Stanislaus. After their discussion, Mr Mozie's advice was: "Ignore that dangerous man Stanislaus." Mr Agomuo did, and recovered.

But one morning, his house-boy reported to him that he had seen a dead male lizard in the backyard. The lizard looked as if it had been cut open, and had a white ribbon round its waist.

Terror sized Mr Agomuo again. He trembled to the Headmaster's house to report the incident. The Headmaster tried in vain to allay his fears.

Mr Agomuo fell ill again, and decided to report the matter to the Supervisor of Schools. The Headmaster and Mr Obiako could not *dissuade* him.

Mr Dewar listened patiently to Mr Agomuo's rigmarole about his illness, his dreams and nightmares, Stanislaus, Mr Okehi, the dead lizard, the Headmaster's lack of sympathy and other disjointed thoughts which came to his mind. Normally, Mr Dewar would have kicked anyone with such a story out of his office. But he had developed a soft spot for Mr Mozie and his school, and knew Mr Agomuo as a keen footballer. He therefore tried to reason with Mr Agomuo and banish his fears. Eventually his patience gave out. He thumped the table frantically, tossing his flowing beard and his red mane of hair, and bawled at the already pathetic-looking teacher: "Out of my sight, you infidel! Where goes your education when you believe that dead lizard can kill a man?"

Mr Agomuo withdrew obediently, unconvinced and unconsoled. He decides that the only person to turn to now was Stanislaus. Little did he know that it was the mischievous Stanilaus who had thrown that harmless lizard into his compound to frighten him?

Mr Dewar for his part decided that such a man should not be left on the staff of that up and coming school, so *full* of promise since the new Headmaster took it over.

10

The Lost Cub

In the last Staff Meeting of the second term, Mr Mozie reviewed the term's achievements. He then outlined three main projects for the third term. These were the introduction of Parents' Day, the reorganization of the House system, and the arrangements for school leavers.

Before they began the discussion on these projects, Miss Chima asked about the plans for volleyball and netball.

The Headmaster took up her question immediately: "We have those matters down for discussion, Miss Chima, but as you have raised the point early, we might as well *dis*pose of it at once. The volleyball court has already been constructed, as you all know, at the far end of the smaller field. Only the bigger boys and girls can play the game, as you appreciate. There is therefore no question of a separate court for girls.

As for the netball, the field is there, the posts are there, and all we need buy are balls. I hope you will be able to show the girls how to make the nets. As you are aware, we are doing our best to keep costs down. Mr Etim here has done a *marvellous* job for the Wolf Cubs, devising everything out of local material apart from their caps, badges and whistles. Is that a fair answer to your question?"

"It is, H.M. Thank you very much," Miss Chima replied.

That over, they went into the planning of the first ever Parents' Day, to be held in October. The parents and their friends would be shown features of the working of the school and there would be displays of the best of the pupils' work in the various subjects. There would be a special hygiene demonstration to show what the parents could do in their own homes.

To make it easier for most pupils to take an active part in the various games, it was proposed to divide them up into four Houses instead of two and for each House to have a colour by which it would be identified. The timing of this reorganisation was contested and it was decided to *postpone* it until the new year. Mr Ibe suggested that when the time came, instead of the one uninspiring, perpetually grey weather-cock on top of the *main* school building, four should be made *and* painted in the House colours, so that the House winning each term's games competition would have its weather-cock 'flying' the following term.

Mr Agomuo's transfer which was affected in the first week of the third term hit his Wanderers Football Club in town more than it hit the school. Mr Dewar had sent in his place a young enthusiastic teacher with a lower

Elementary Teacher's Certificate, like Miss Chima had. The Headmaster pushed Miss Chima another rung up, giving her Mr Agomuo's former class, Standard Four, while the new teacher took Standard Three. Miss Chima's Standard Three pupils were decidedly unhappy, but, before she left them, she cheered them with the promise: "If you work hard you will be in my class next year. Isn't it better to have you for a whole year next year instead of for only one more term this year?"

"It is, Miss," they cheered.

A few tongues *wagged* that Mr Mozie had done it again getting rid of the teachers he did not like. But this gossip was among Mr Agomuo's football fans in town, and did not bother Mr Mozie.

The new teacher settled down and fitted in perfectly. The school went *like clock*-work. Mr Etim's Wolf Cubs worked for their profi*ciency* certificates in athletics, climbing, tracking, signalling, swimming and cooking. Mr Brown-Wilcox, the music master, prepared the school choir for Parents' Day and for the annual district singing contest. Three boys went in for the Hope Waddell entrance examination and two were invited to the interview for final selection. Parents' Day came and was an *astounding* success. Nothing seemed capable of going wrong as the school headed for the final examinations, the General Knowledge competition, the Christmas concert, and the holidays.

The Wolf Cubs had planned a hike with their leader, Mr Etim. They set out as usual on Saturday morning, their haversacks bulging. They had already thoroughly explored the nearby woodlands, and Akela (as they called Mr Etim) decided that they should venture into the river valley which lay in really thick jungle. The boys were jubilant and raised the chant: "We'll D-O-B! D-O-B! D-O-B! D-O-B!"

Bassey Okon had developed into one of the ablest young leaders and Ishmael, who was in Bassey's group, was also a very keen Wolf Cub. He had always loved outdoor life. Hik*ing thrilled* him. Nothing daunted him, and while he was around, no valley, cave or undergrowth was too dangerous to explore and no tree or rock was too difficult to climb.

When they reached a point of the river where it was joined by a stream flowing into it, one of the boys asked Mr Etim: "Akela, is it true that water is warmer when a stream joins a river?"

"You are a Wolf Cub, Jonah, find out for yourself."

"Akcla, can we swim here then?" The boy asked.

"Certainly."

"Hurrah!" The boys shouted. They unslung their haversacks, stripped and went in, splash!

splash! one after another. The first few reported that the water was truly warm.

Mr Etim saw that there was a good stretch of water there, and announced that he would be holding proficiency tests in swimming. He took out his notebook and called out the names of those who had applied to be examined, then ordered the rest out of the water.

"*Hurrah!*" *The* boys went in a splash!
splash! one after the *other.*

He instructed the group leader to take their groups climbing until lunch time when he would give the Wolf Cub a call for all to assemble.

That lunch was never taken.

When Mr Etim called the assembly was *brisk* and orderly, each Cub returning the appropriate call as he hurried back to base. Mr Etim was impressed. The boys were coming on, he felt. But when they started unpacking their lunches, someone observed that Jonah was missing. It was true. His haversack was there, but no Jonah. The unpacking stopped. Mr Etim first took a look down the river just to make sure, and then let out call after call, first gently, then at the top of his voice. All he got back was an *echo*. Some of the boys tried to help him *by* calling themselves, but he hushed them. The rest of the afternoon was spent in an organized combing of the surrounding area and of the river banks, but without success.

It was a silent and bedraggled group who headed for home just before sunset. Mr Etim had never had to cope with such a serious situation.

Gloom descended on the school and the village that weekend. To the village-folk, death was a terrible thing, and in the face of it, their goodness, *demeanour* and composure broke down. Many uncharitable things were said about the Headmaster and Mr Etim. On the spot, they became *villains*. The one redeeming feature in the whole pathetic situation was that Amanzu people were never given to violence. Further, that great man, Matthew, stepped in as he had always done in any difficult situation. First he asserted that there was no evidence that the missing boy was dead and that instead of assuming it, search parties should be organized, and people sent to neighbouring villages to ask about the boy in case he had lost his way in the forest and wandered into another village. Then he emphasized that the teachers were not to blame for what, if anything, would be an accident.

The boy was not found that night and the search parties stood by to try again at dawn. Stanislaus, ever ready to help, waited with the rest of the people.

There were few able-bodied men at the church service the following morning. The Catechist devoted the service to praying for the missing boy. All the men were out on the search, but nothing came of it except a deeper gloom. More searches were planned.

As there was no Police Post in Amanzu, *Mr* Mozie had to ride to Umuahia to report the situation first to Mr Dewar and then to the Police post in Amanzu, The boy's body was not found, if indeed he had drowned, and a funeral was out of the question.

It was very difficult to be bold or unemotional in such circumstances in a small and almost close community. But time marched on, and Monday morning came. The school bells rang, the school assembled, and lessons were resumed. Life still had to be lived.

On Monday afternoon, *pandemonium* broke out when pupils saw the missing boy walking into the school premises with two *stalwart* men and a woman who they did not know. Discipline was out of the question now. Windows and dwarf walls were jumped; the strangers were surrounded; pupils *ran helter skelter*; some ran into the village to report the big news. Soon the school compound swarmed with village-folk, and the strangers had to retell their story for each wave of new arrivals. They told how the boy was picked up from the lower reaches of the river near their own village; how he floated on his back and they took him for dead; how they pressed *all the* water out of his ballooned stomach and took him home; how he recovered slowly and it was not until Sunday evening that he could tell them where he came from; and how they came upstream to bring the boy home. They gave credit to the woman, who had spotted the boy while she was washing her clothes on the bank and raised the alarm.

The *missing* boy *walking* into the *school* premises

That was the end of school for the day. It was also the end of the market when news got there. The general rejoicing completely swamped the village. Jonah's rescuers were not allowed to return home that evening. They were the honoured guests of Jonah's parents and of the entire village. Gifts poured into the house for them. The pupils could now afford to release the song they had been suppressing: 'Jonah in the fish belly'.

A few days later, the Police 'hurried' to Amanzu with orders "... to investigate the case of the missing boy, and institute a search".

11

Lost to a New Life

The scare of Jonah's near-*tragedy* did not make Mr Mozie *swerve* from his struggle to enrich the lives of his pupils and of the village with new activities. But perhaps it served the useful purpose of reminding him that one twist *of fate* could bring down all his achievements *like a pack of cards*.

The closing weeks of the third term were crammed with activities. The school had a bumper harvest from its new farm and its contribution to the harvest thanksgiving service was *tremendous*. The *bazaar* which followed raised so much money that the Committee was very happy to vote a substantial amount to the school's fund.

An additional celebration was a school feast suggested by Mr Obiako and readily approved by the Headmaster. It was organized entirely by the pupils, each House planning its own *menu.* The teachers were the honoured guests of each House in turn, and a more pleasant evening could not have been imagined.

At each table, each teacher was given a card on which to award marks out of ten for the dishes which he tasted. They were not required to write their names on the cards. At the same time, unknown to the teachers, the amount of food each ate at each table was recorded.

After the feast, which was held in the Assembly Hall, all the teachers' cards were collected and handed over to the Headmaster to add up the marks.

The unofficial title for the best cooks went to B House. Mr Mozie *paid tribute* to B House for winning, but what pleased him was the suggestion by the pupils that the quality of their cooking should be assessed. This assured him that the desire *to excel* had taken root in the school.

"Perhaps we should present B House with a pot to mark the occasion," he added.

The Head Boy, who had made his own assessment from the record of the student judges at each table, thanked the Headmaster and the other members of staff for accepting their invitation. "We have no doubt," he went on, "that our amateur cooking cannot match the rich dishes you are used to in *your* own houses. Our only prayer is that *none of* you should wake up with an upset stomach. *I* shall end by announcing the re*sult* of our contest for the best eater on the *staff*. The best eater among the teachers is *our* Standard Three teacher. Give him a hand!"

The school responded with thunderous applause.

"And here is a prize for the winner, two of choicest dishes for him to take home.

Those were the ones he did most justice to during the feast," "The Head Boy concluded.

No one saw anything but fun in the announcement, and everyone joined heartily in the laughter.

One rather sad note at the end of the term was the warning from the Reverend Mr Jones that Miss Hill of the Girls' Demonstration School proposed to recall Miss Chima *to* her school now that it was almost back to its *full capacity* again. Mr Mozie in particular, and the staff in general, dreaded the prospect. Miss Chima had been an angel in their midst. She had given the *Headmaster* her complete and *unflinching support*. She had been a wonderful *inspiration* to all the girls,

Chima might be recalled any day. With the men's programme he was more cautious, because of the recent trouble about Jonah.

Dr. Bankole-Bright, who was in charge of the Government hospital in Umuahia, heard from Mr Dewar about the Headmaster's work in Amanzu, particularly the work among the women. This impressed him so much that he came down to Amanzu to see for himself. He was *not* disappointed. He had been impressed by the school when he came to the opening of the football field the previous year, and he was even more impressed now. One immediate benefit to the school of this visit was the promise to examine the pupil in batches when he came on tour to the nearby dispensary.

While the fear of the loss of Miss Chima still *hovered* over the Headmaster, he lost an equally loyal and a more influential friend. Matthew, the able committee leader, had lived in Amanzu for so long that few people remembered, or even knew, that he came from Amasa (meaning seven villages), a vigorous but dwindling town whose fame rested on the story of its boisterous people's resistance to British *pacification* at the end of the nineteenth century. Matthew's uncle had *been* paramount Chief for over twenty years. He had died recently, and it was Matthew's *due* and his duty to become Paramount Chief, *succession* being *by* the oldest member of the ruling family rather than *by* *direct* descent. Amazu gave Matthew a right royal send-*off*. The women wept as they smothered his wife Martha with gifts. Matthew asked that one of his younger sons, still in school, should live with Mr *Mozie* until the end of the year, more as a mark of their friendship than for any practical reasons.

The next idea which occurred to Mr Mozie was the introduction of a small library in the school. The children read only the prescribed readers for their respective classes and one or, at the most, two supplementary readers. The children now wanted more books *to* read. The Wolf Cub movement had made many of them more enterprising and more *inquisi*tive. They asked continual questions in and out of class.

He decided he was not going to seek official financial support for this project. He got his members of staff to regard it as one thing they were going to do *for* the school on their own, and convinced them that their efforts would be remembered many years after they had left the school. He suggested a collection of little paperbacks and abridged editions of standard works to which more books could be added as time went on. If they got it started, he would consider asking for donations of money or books from educated people in the town. Mr Mozie carried them as he knew he would, with the support of Mr Obiako, Miss Chima and Mr Ibe assured even before he started. They raised money for the building of their 'monument' of books. A carpenter built two cupboards for the school at a *nominal* cost. The library scheme was under way.

But before long the calamity of Miss Chima's departure hit the school. It came from an unexpected quarter. Dr. Bankole Bright had first heard about Miss Chima from Mr Dewar, his neighbour and friend at Umuahia. When the doctor came to see the school and village, following Mr Dewar's glowing account of the Headmaster's work in the school, the Headmaster and Mr Obiako and the women whom he spoke to all affirmed that Miss Chima was an outstanding girl. They all referred to her intelligence, her goodness, and her kindness. In fact some of the women used the word 'angel' freely.

The doctor felt that such was ideally suited for the medical profession. He asked Miss Chima if she would like to be trained as a nurse in England. The idea came to her as a surprise, but she told Dr. Bankole-Bright that she would write and ask her father. The doctor told her about his own family and their interest in the profession. His father was a retired doctor in Freetown, Sierra Leone. His own sister, Claudia, trained as a nurse in the same hospital in England where he and their father before him had qualified as doctors. His sister now worked in Lagos. The youngest member of his family, his daughter, aged one year, would one day be joining them. He amused her by saying that when he wrote to the Matron of that Hospital in England announcing the birth of his daughter, he added as a footnote that the Matron should book a *place* for the little girl eighteen years hence!

Miss Chima smiled. He told her that while awaiting her father's reply, he would write to his sister in Lagos about her. *If* her father agreed, he would then write to the Matron in England.

Mr Mozie looked on with the greatest discomfort. What could he do?

Miss Claudia Olive Bankole-Bright, S.R.N., was more dynamic and vivacious than her brother.

When she read his description of his marvellous discovery, she took a fortnight's leave and travelled immediately to Umuahia to see *for* herself. She came down to Amanzu with her brother. She wore the fashionable clothes of the period, a mid-calf length silk dress, with hat, high-heeled shoes, handbag and umbrella, all tastefully matched.

Amazu had never seen anyone so elegant. The pupils were *seething with* curiosity.

Miss Bankole-Bright thought Miss Chima was as good as her brother's letter had sounded, and more. He had not referred to her good looks. Had her father replied? He had not.

"Well then, we have got to go and see him right away. If the mountain cannot go to Mohammed, Mohammed must go to the mountain, isn't that it, Bobby?" she asked, turning to her brother. He smiled.

Miss *Bankole-Bright*.

It was Friday. Mr Mozie agreed to excuse Miss Chima for the rest of the day. They drove off in the doctor's car, first to Umuahia, and then to Bende since there was no motorable shortcut.

Poor *Mr Chima* was overcome *by* the sight of Miss Bankole or Bola Bright, but she soon put everyone at their ease. The younger children ran out to hug their sister. Miss Bankole-Bright soon got down to business. What Mr Chima *had* to say was just what she wanted to hear. He told them how he had started to reply *to* his daughter's letter three times, and each time he was lost for words to continue. He had consequently Law decided to leave the matter until she returned for the Easter holidays.

"But we can't wait. Daddy. This girl is too good, too precious to waste her life and talents. She is a born nurse. She ought to be a nurse," Miss Bankole-Bright said firmly. Mr Chima still hedged, hemming and humming in unconcealed hesitation.

The doctor whispered into his sister's ear that perhaps the man's greatest fears were financial.

"Ah!" she gasped. "And another point, Daddy, this thing is not going to cost you a penny. My brother and I are intensely interested in Com. I will personally guarantee her fare to and from England. My brother and I will see to her pocket money so that she will be happy in England. She will also get an allowance from her hospital as soon as she starts her training.

"By the way, Daddy, when I say my brother is interested in Com, please don't misunderstand me." Miss Bankole-Bright rushed on. "He has exactly the same interest as I have her welfare. He does not want to marry Com, 'and that's not because she is not beautiful. She is *gorgeous*. But my brother already has one wife, five sons and one little daughter... a handful you will agree!" Everyone laughed.

Next Miss Bankole-Bright turned to Mrs. Chima and soon she was floored just *as* her husband had been floored, by sheer Gun fire'. How could anyone refuse this lady anything, even one's daughter?

Things moved fast after that. Miss Chima tendered her resignation. Miss Bankole Bright paid the Mission one month's salary in *lieu* of notice. She fired *off* letters to the Matron in England, and at the end of her local leave, she whisked Miss Chima off to Lagos to prepare for her trip.

12

Disaster Strikes

The second major pillar of Mr Mozie's *edifice* had gone. He did his utmost to keep his poise and maintain his boat, the school, *on an even keel.*

Things went normally until June. Then the *avalanche* of disasters, difficulties and disappointments continued. First, Mr Brown-Wilcox, the music master, who had lifted the school *from the doldrums* of croaking to the winning of their first singing contest, was in trouble with one of the choir girls.

Her parents took her from the school and sent her away from the village.

The *rumpus* which stirred up was *still thick in the air* when a dispute broke out over the new piece of land on which the school farm stood. The farm, with the crops in midseason, was seized by one of the sons of the village head. He then went on to *sue* his father for selling to the school a piece of land which belonged to the family. Stanislaus was at hand to help the litigant prepare the case against his father.

The last thing Mr Mozie wanted was to see his school dragged into a court case. So immediately he heard of the trouble, he went to Umuahia to report to Mr Dewar and he sent Mr Obiako to see Matthew in Ama-asa.

Chief Mathew used his influence to get the case withdrawn from the court in Bende and offered to help with the settlement.

He came to Amanzu, and it emerged at the peace meeting that the village head, Chief Idigo, had actually *instigated* the *litigation* himself because he wanted the school to pay him every year for the use of the land. When Mr Offor, the former Headmaster, had farmed on the same piece of land, he had paid rent to the village head. But Chief Matthew and Mr Obiako had pleaded with the chief to give the land free to the school. He had done so, but had seen recently that the yield from the farm was so great that he wanted the school to pay him for the use of the land.

Chief Matthew told the village head that it was uncharitable of him to take money for that piece of land from a school which is doing so much good in his village. The Chief *conferred* further with Mr Mozie who offered to pay rent in kind at the end of each harvest season.

The greedy chief consulted his son, and they demanded: 'Cash payment *or* return the land.'

Mr Mozie knew that Mr Dewar was not prepared to be involved in land disputes of any kind unless the actual school compound was involved. He also knew that he could afford to pay £5 being demanded by the village head.

The farm had yielded much more than the previous year. He explained this to Chief Matthew and they then told the ungrateful village head that his demand would be met.

Even in the classroom, the ground gained was slipping away again. They had lost Miss Chima, and Mr Dewar was unable to secure a replacement before he left for England on leave.

Only Mr Obiako strove to cheer up and *bolster* his young enthusiastic Headmaster. The old man was like a father to him, but Mr Mozie was *despondent.* Nothing seemed to go right now. He wondered whether there was any sense in striving to do good, or to work hard, when life could bring such sudden twists of fate.

But the avalanche had not finished yet.

The Wolf Cub movement, that great dream which was expected to become *a* beacon of light, misfired again, this time really *catastrophically.* It was August, the time of the brief break in the wet season, known as the 'August break. One of the public holidays was being celebrated on a Thursday, so there was no school.

Mr Etim thought it would be a good idea to exploit the 'August break' in an attempt to boost the *morale* of the boys which was evidently at *a* low *ebb* on account of the troubles in the school. He took his Wolf Cubs out on an afternoon hike, but did not venture far into the forest. They started off in the woodlands near the school, dividing up into groups for various activities.

Ishmael, the boy with the innate sense of direction and *flair* for outdoor life, had reinforced himself with a compass. Without the instrument he could never be confused in any bush or faulted as far as sense of direction was concerned. With a compass, therefore, he could be expected to perform even greater feats.

Once in the bush with the rest, Ishmael took one of his friends, a skinny, un enterprising boy with the unbefitting name of Goliath, and they went off on their own. One of those they used was planted for signalling, on a certain spot. Ishmael drew a plan on the ground *for* his friend to see. Using the compass, they would walk 500 steps north, turned at a right angle and walk 500 steps to the east. He reckoned that they should arrive back at the pennant if the compass worked correctly.

No one knew how far they had walked or in which direction they were heading, when a tropical storm broke. Ishmael did not know what terrible happenings his compass (less reliable than his innate sense) was bound to bring about.

The storm broke with very little warming. It was as if the heavens were opened suddenly. The torrents were blinding from the start. The trees offered no cover. It flashed and thundered.

Tropical storms were not new to Mr Etim or to his Wolf Cubs. But this particular one had something *sinister* about it from the start. It was as if it swallowed one up. It was frightening. Mr Etim stood for some time with the group of Cubs he was testing. Whistling for the rest of the Pack was useless as a whistle would not have carried a message in that *deluge*. Calling was equally futile. Searching for others was unwise. Besides, they were reasonably near home, and all of them should be able to find their way back even in the rain. So Mr Etim took the boys back to school.

There they joined another group of Cubs who had found their way home earlier and were singing in one of the classrooms. Returning to their homes was out of the question because Akela had not dismissed them. Besides, most of the roads were flooded and hazardous.

The two groups exchanged accounts of their adventures. They felt confident that the other Cubs would soon find their way home. There was a short lull in the storm. It soon began raining again with all its ferocity, but the break had allowed some cubs to find their way out of the forest. In the still blinding rain, a group of them arrived, *soaked* to the skin, cold, but cheerful. Another group arrived half an hour later and the pack appeared to be complete.

The anxious Mr Etim asked: "Is everyone back now?"

"I think everyone is back," someone answered.

"Jonah here?" Mr Etim asked.

"Yes, Akela.*"*

*"*Bassey*?"*

"Yes, Akela.*"*

"Ishmael? *Is* Ishmael back?"

There was no answer.

"That miserable Ishmael again. He is always causing trouble," someone grumbled.

"Who was with Ishmael? In which group was he?" Mr Etim asked.

"He was in my group, Akela," Bassey answered. "He was with Goliath."

"When did you lose sight of them?"

"You know what Ishmael is like, Akela. Once he is in the bush, he feels like a bird released from a cage. When we got into the bush, he said he was going to find out whether his compass worked."

"Now you, you and you, run to Ishmael's home and see if the *blighter* has gone home on his own," Mr Etim ordered.

"Yes, Akela."

"Make sure you don't drown yourselves on the way."

"Yes, Akela."

Meanwhile the singing continued. Nobody could imagine that Ishmael could get lost.

They felt sure that he would either come back while Bassey and his companions were away or that they would bring him back.

The evening wore on. Ishmael and Goliath did not arrive nor did Bassey and his companions.

It was getting dark when the messengers returned, running. It was a surprise that they had any energy left.

"Any news?" Mr Etim asked hopefully.

"None, Akela. Ishmael's parents said they had not seen him. On our way back we met Goliath's father and he asked if his son was with us."

The matter was now serious. Night had fallen. Mr Etim went to the Headmaster to report this new trouble.

"No, not again, Mr Etim! Not another missing Cub. How are we going to explain this to the townspeople?"

Mr Etim had no answer. There was nothing to do but to mount an immediate search. Mr Mozie alerted Mr Obiako and all the other teachers. He also sent for the new Committee leader, Peter, and asked for all able-bodied men to be summoned to comb the surrounding forest without delay. Mr Dewar's warning about the people's reaction in the *face of* disaster rang *in* Mr Mozie's ears, but *he* steadied himself and organized and led the search party.

The rain had ceased. The party assembled where the Wolf Cubs had assembled before breaking up into groups. Then they fanned out in different directions. It was like a torchlight parade but with no element of merriment. Small incidents had already strained the relationship between the school and the people. Failure that night would be the last straw. And failure seemed assured as the rain came again. The first gust of wind put out many of the bush candles.

Then the rain made further progress impossible.

No one slept well in Amanzu that night, except perhaps the little children. Many of the townspeople kept a vigil with the teachers in the school compound, ready to resume the search during the night. The rain did not give them the chance until dawn.

As soon as there was light, the search went on in earnest.

When Ishmael was found, he was slumped over a large tree very far from home. He was cold, wet and muddy, his hand, face and body bruised from a night-long *gallant,* but futile, effort to push away the fallen tree which pinned down his friend Goliath.

Ishmael was rushed to the nearby Mission dispensary still unconscious. Sawyers were needed to free the body of the dead boy, Goliath.

That looked like the end of school for the term. There was no Matthew now to control the people's emotions. The crowd ordered that even though the term had two more weeks to go, they had had enough. They set up barriers to ensure that the order was obeyed.

Stanislaus, who had been very active in the search party, went into action again, this time at the express invitation of the people rather than at his own suggestion. His mammoth dictionaries were brought out and dusted. He had been out of big business for quite some time. He was raring to go. He already knew what to write, but still listened to the mob pouring out their venom on Mr Mozie, Mr Etim and the school.

In the petition, Stanislaus described Mr Mozie as a dreamer, in accord with his name, Joseph, the dreamer. Then he accused him of turning the school and the village upside down, ruining the children by abolishing flogging, pampering the pupils and inciting then to insult their parents and elders through the so-called adult education scheme, appropriating land, exposing the children to moral danger, transferring teachers whom he hated, allowing the only woman teacher to be spirited away to England, forming a movement which nearly succeeded in drowning one of the pupils (Jonah) and which finally succeeded in crushing one to death (Goliath).

Every conceivable mishap which had happened since Mr Mozie took over as Headmaster was recalled. His immediate dismissal was demanded as well as that of Mr Etim. The petition also called for the abolition of the Wolf Cub Pack and the Adult Education Scheme.

Finally the petition called for the return of the former Headmaster who was referred to as "our beloved and highly esteemed friend, Mr Augustus H.G. Offor, a man who is one with the people, a man of discipline and a man of

God; the only man who can redeem the Amanzu
Central School and restore its lost glory and
tranquillity".

Copies of the petition were posted to the
Reverend William Jones, School Manager; to
the new Supervisor of Schools, Mr Jackson; to
the District Officer *in* Umuahia and to the
Resident in Owerri. Delegations were also sent,
bearing copies of the petition to these same
officials.

13

The Truth is Revealed

The worst day was the first day. Mr Mozie decided that he had to think fast and act swiftly. He believed that the real test of a man was in a crisis. He was determined not to give up the school. The mob would have to take his life first.

First he called Mr Obiako, the wise old Church teacher, and told him what he intended to do. The old man had *implicit* confidence in the Headmaster and supported him in his determination to fight. He cautioned, however, that everything should be done to avoid *incensing* the people to violence.

"Blood must not be spilt over the work of God. The unfortunate boy's death was an accident, pure and simple," he concluded.

a full Staff fed ex Mr Mozie s

Meeting, and after thanking them for their loyalty and support in the past, urged them to stand by him in the school's hour of trial. He was fighting, not to save himself or them, but to save their cherished school from the understandable but blind *emotional* outburst of the people of Amanzu.

The staff realized it could be very risky pitching the school against the community, but they shared the Headmaster's belief that truth and right will triumph in the end. They therefore gave him their support.

Peter, the new Committee leader, did not have Matthew's imposing personality, but he was equally loyal to Mr Mozie. At the request of the Headmaster, he summoned a Committee meeting that morning. Mr Mozie took Mr Obiako along with him to the meeting.

After expressing his deep sorrow at Goliath's death, the Headmaster told the meeting that the choice before them was between burying the Amanzu Central School with the dead pupil, or allowing the school to stand as a monument to the boy who gave his life, and to others, including the members of the Committee, who gave their sweat in the building of the school.

But the Committee was not *swayed*. What was clear to many of them was that many things had been going wrong with the school since Mr Offor left, and if the Headmaster did not recognize the death of a pupil as a disaster, there must be something wrong with his head. It was often said, one of them added dryly: "That too much reading spoils the head"

Peter and some other members saw the Headmaster's point and tried to win over the others.

The split in the Committee encouraged Mr Mozie. Since there was no *unanimous* opposition from the Committee, there was still hope. Provided the split in opinion was reflected in the whole parish, he had a chance.

He took Mr Obiako and Peter along to see Goliath's parents, the leaders of the Women's Guild, and then the village head, Chief Idigo.

There was grief in Goliath's home but no show of violence. The meeting with the Women's Guild leaders was not very comforting. Their relationship with the bachelor Headmaster had not been cordial as he had seemed out of touch with women's problems. They spoke as if each of them was herself Goliath's mother.

When Mr Mozie got to Chief Idigo's house, he found the chief *adamant* in his view that Mr

Mozie had brought a string of disasters to the school and the people of Amanzu.

Mr Mozie was not dismayed. He had completed what he wanted to do at Amanzu that day. In the afternoon, he rode to Umuahia to report to Mr Jackson.

"Hello, Joseph, *you look* worried. Sit down. Now tell me what is worrying you.'

"I am sorry to inform you that we have had a very bad accident in the school. A pupil died in a terrible storm yesterday evening. He was a Wolf Cub, and was out hiking with the other Cubs when the accident occurred."

"This is tragic news, Joseph. But a storm is an act of God and accidents are inevitable at times."

"Yes, sir, but the people of Amanzu and indeed our people in general, are too awed by death to accept it as accidental. The people of Amanzu are *up in* arms against me, and against the young teacher who took the boys out hiking, and against the whole school."

"I am aware of that, Joseph."

"Are you?" Mr Mozie was taken aback. "I am indeed. I already have a copy of their petition, which was apparently written this morning and delivered by two angry-looking men who called here just before noon."

"So they have already petitioned. That Stanislaus!" Mr Mozie sighed.

"They have made many charges against and they have demanded the recall of the former Headmaster, Mr Offor," Mr Jackson went on.

"I thought they would. What *is* going to happen, sir?"

"What is going to happen is that you will return to your school and you will continue to be Headmaster until the charges made against you are probed. As Supervisor of Schools, I am not going to abandon one of our Mission schools to a mob. They have apparently sent copies of their petition to the Reverend Jones and to the District Officer and the Resident. I am surprised that they forgot the Lieutenant-Governor and the Governor, not that I see what these government gentlemen have to do with our schools."

"I am pleased that there will be an investigation. I am quite prepared to stand down as Headmaster or to leave the place altogether if my presence will be a source of embarrassment to the investigators.

"Nonsense. You'll stay at your post. I shall go to Port Harcourt to see the Reverend Jones about the whole matter."

"But the risk of violence will remain unless they hear from you or from the Reverend Jones very soon. I thought that a visit to the place for a few days would dispel the and the posting of some policemen 'danger of a riot at this critical period. It may sound high-handed or menacing bringing in the Police, but they can be there under the guise of investigating the death of the pupil rather than an eye on the people," suggested Mr Mozie.

Mr Jackson thought over the suggestions for a minute: "Okay, I'll come to your school tomorrow morning. Gather the parishioners and other interested people in the Assembly Hall and I will speak to them. I shall consider your other suggestion."

"Thank you, sir. I shall do as you say. I'm not sure whether this is the time and place to present these letters, but *I* have here with me a letter written to me from England by a former teacher of ours, one Miss Comfort Chima, and also some letters written to the girl by the former Headmaster of the school, Mr Offor, and by his wife. You may find the contents of these letters helpful."

Mr Jackson took the letters from Mr Mozie without looking at them. "Goodbye, Joseph," he said, offering his hand.

"Goodbye, sir. We shall expect you tomorrow.

The sight of the Policemen in a village always excited much interest and *speculation.* Two arrived in the school compound at about half past seven the next morning. They went to the Headmaster's house and stayed for nearly half an hour. Two other policemen went to Chief Idigo's house, and after that, they interviewed a number of people in the village. They told the Chief that they had come to investigate the death of the schoolboy, but that the District Officer's orders were that the Central School must not be closed by force and that there must be no rioting in Amanzu.

The people had mixed feelings about the *turn of events,* but against uniformed policemen and orders from the District Officer, they could do nothing. They hoped that the investigations would end in the arrest and removal of Mr Mozie and the other teacher whom they believed had caused the death of Goliath.

The policemen ordered some men to remove the roadblocks put up the previous day at the height of the people's anger. They also urged people to send their children back to school according to the District Officer's orders.

The** Church hall was *full as if it* was a ***Sundays

School attendance was poor that morning. No one was surprised. Mr Mozie took the Assembly quickly and asked the teachers to *go* on with their classes while he prepared for Mr Jackson's arrival.

The Church Hall was full as if it was a Sunday. The atmosphere was subdued, and tense. The Supervisor of Schools had never addressed the parishioners before, and they wondered what he would say to them. They wondered when the end of all the troubles caused by the Headmaster would come.

Soon the sound of Mr Jackson's motorcycle was heard. He arrived accompanied by a clerk from his office. Mr Mozie met him at the South Gate, introduced the other teachers briefly and sent them back to their classes to keep the pupils occupied.

The Headmaster took Mr Jackson straight into the hall, the clerk walking behind them. He introduced the Supervisor briefly and then sat down.

Mr Jackson spoke to the gathering, using his clerk as interpreter: "My brothers and Sisters in Christ, *I* share your deep grief in the death of the little schoolboy who died two y days ago. May his innocent soul rest in peace of them was still required to give evidence. When the commission moved to Umuahia, the chairman's station, they invited Mr and Mrs. Offor, two former teachers of the school, Mr Okehi and Mr Agomuo, and Paramount Chief Matthew from Ama-asa. All attended and gave evidence.

The Commission wanted to interview Stanislaus again in connection with the earlier petition on which Mr Offor had laid great emphasis, but Stanislaus was not available. He had been arrested earlier that week and charged with some postal offences. One was Posting letters with used stamps which he dipped in *diluted* lime juice in an attempt to erase previous postal markings; the other was stealing postal orders which were being sent to or sent by clients for whom he read or wrote letters. The Commission did not miss him unduly. He had said enough in his first interview in Amanzu to leave the Commission in no doubt as to who was the moving spirit behind the petition he wrote for the mob on the death of Goliath.

When the report was ready, the Commissioners sent it through the chairman to the Reverend Mr Jones in Port Harcourt.

14

The Villain of the Story

When the Reverend Mr Jones read the Commission's report he was startled and saddened by the story which it told him of the happenings at Amanzu.

The next day he sent for Mr Offor, who travelled to Port Harcourt knowing what to expect from the Manager. He went to the office at the appointed time and the Manager's clerk announced him.

"Come in, Headmaster," Reverend Jones called,

Mr. Offor *shuffled* in, looking a shadow of his majestic self.

"Good morning, Headmaster. Sit down. Have you had a good journey?"

"Yes, sir."

"You probably know, Headmaster, why I sent for you." Mr Offor made no response.

"It breaks my heart," Reverend Jones continued, "to see a sound and sober man like a man of iron discipline crack up and you, falter under pressure. We once dreamt of a Reverend Augustus Offor joining us to build a strong church here, but that will not now be.

"Did you write these letters to Miss Chima saying you would do anything to return to Amanzu?"

"I did, sir."

"Did your wife write similar letters to Miss Chima in connection with her trade with the commercial houses in Amanzu?"

"I believe she did, sir."

"Did you *conspire* with that ex-convict Stanislaus, whom you once *despised,* to embarrass Mr Mozie by petition writing at the slightest opportunity?"

"I did, sir."

"You know one Chief Idigo, don't you?

"I do, sir."

"Did you conspire with him to embarrass Mr Mozie by *litigation* over a piece of land used for the school farm?

"I did not, sir. I paid rent on the said piece of land when I was at Amanzu, but whoever *insinuated* that I had a hand in Chief Idigo's litigation was *letting his imagination run away with him.*"

"All right. Is Mr Brown-Wilcox, a businessman and musician, related to your wife?"

"He is, sir."

"Was his illicit love affair with a school girl planned by your wife in order to show how low morals in the school had fallen since you left that school?"

"I wouldn't know, sir. Anything is possible."

"Would you admit that one thing drove you to these blunders, your wife's insistence on returning to re-establish her business in Amanzu?"

"I do, sir."

"It is sad, Mr Offor. In a court of law, they could probably talk of *extenuating circumstances* and take into consideration your admission of your faults. Our code is much less lenient. Children and church men and prospective church men and women are watching us and our every act every day. We cannot afford the luxury of doubtful behaviour. I have no alternative but to terminate your appointment."

The Reverend Mr Jones sent for Mr Jackson and instructed him on how to give the report of the Commission of Inquiry to the people of Amanzu.

Mr Jackson sent for Mr Mozie to acquaint him with the *turn* of *events*.

"I am glad, Joseph, that you decided to stand up to these people. *I* hope your school will now go on from strength to strength," Mr Jackson concluded.

"I have no words to thank you for your kindness and support, without which success would have been impossible. I am sure that the pupils and the good people of Amanzu would like to thank you too."

"Goodbye, Joseph, and enjoy what is left of your holidays."

"Goodbye, sir."

www.ingramcontent.com/pod-product-compliance
Lightning Source LLC
Chambersburg PA
CBHW060418310726
48976CB00003B/1096